BULLY BUSTER
Journal

by Annie Winston

Illustrations by Gary Locke

CEDAR GATE
PUBLISHING

3508 French Park Drive Ste. 1, Edmond, Oklahoma 73034 • cedargatepublishing.com

Winston, Annie.
  Bully Buster Journal

Summary: Seventh grader, Andy Jones, is tormented by the school bully until his mysterious uncle shows up with a battle plan from an ancient book.

Copyright ® 2020 by Cedar Gate Publishing.
ISBN 978-0-9997117-7-4

Text copyright ® 2020 by Annie Winston
Illustrations copyright ® 2020 by Gary Locke
Edited by Holden Hill & Publishing Director Randy Allsbury
Design and layout by Dale Gehris

First Edition

Illustrations created and prepared in digital format by Gary Locke.
The text of this book is set in 12 point Leftovers.
Font licensed from Font Diner, Inc.
Cover illustrated by Gary Locke.
Cover and layout design by Dale Gehris, Fair Grove, Missouri.

Printed in the United States of America.

MEET THE CHARACTERS

Andy Jones
Awkward sixth grader.
This is his journal.

Tommy Mugersnot
Andy's archnemesis.

George Jones
He loves ice cream
and grasshoppers!

Buckles
Belongs to Andy.
"Smartest dog
in the world!"

Uncle Dug
Andy's mysterious,
long-lost uncle.

Mom
She works hard
to support Andy
and George.

Flynn
Best friend to
Andy and loves
making videos.

Aunt Gertie
She's eccentric
and tough.

Mr. Bullard
He knows a
lot about the
universe.

Prudence Glummer
Andy's biggest
fan!

Dedicated to

the kid who knows what it is like
to be bullied and is maybe just a little curious
about the best way to bust a bully.

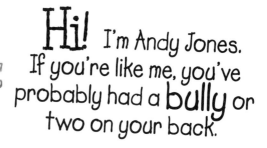

Hi! I'm Andy Jones.
If you're like me, you've probably had a **bully** or two on your back.

If so, you're going to want to read my journal. I wouldn't have kept it if it hadn't been for my Aunt Gertie, who's really my great-aunt. She's my mom's, mom's sister who has had sixty-three more birthdays than me.

Aunt Gertie is always getting mad at me for spending too much time on the "electronic rectangle" (her name for an iPad). I tell her I'm not goofing around gaming; I'm usually on a doodling app practicing my drawing. But Aunt Gertie had her own ideas about what I should be doing. Almost everything is a time-waster in her opinion, except for reading a book or putting a real pencil or pen in your hand. When she saw my spelling test, she got really upset and said the way I wrote my letters looked like a bunch of slithering snakes.

It was her **Texan** way of telling me my **sloppy** handwriting was in need of serious help.

1

She bought me a journal and told me to write and doodle in it every day "to keep the snakes away." Aunt Gertie also believed with all of her big Texas heart that the journal would be good for my soul if I started writing down everything that happened to me.

So that's what I did. Sometimes I got carried away and wrote a lot, which is amazing since I don't normally like putting thoughts or feely stuff on paper. I journaled about my struggle with the worst bully in the universe, Tommy Mugersnot, and how I tried to convince my best friend Flynn to make a video to save my life.

I also **wrote** about some awesome stargazing and getting to know my Uncle Dug when he came to visit for the first time.

Uncle Dug slept on the bottom bunk in my room, and, after the lights were off, he would tell my little brother George and me a radical story about an ancient dude who knew the incredible secret of how to bust a bully. You'll only find out what it is if you read my journal. I hope you do, and that you like it and my doodling. Mom loved it, but all moms love what their kids do. Well, as long as they're not getting into trouble, that is. Aunt Gertie told me I did a great job of chasing the snakes away, which means she's now off my back about my handwriting. When I read my journal to Buckles, my dog, he wagged his stumpy tail and listened.

But I'm pretty sure it was only because I kept giving him pieces of **beef** jerky.

Your Friend,
Andy Jones
Sixth Grader
Woodside Junior High
Great Barrington, Massachusetts
President of the first Bully Busters Club

Clobbered

I admit it. I don't know much. I'm only eleven. But I do know what it's like to be clobbered by bullies. I'm a sixth grader at Woodside Junior High. I've lived three days of horribleness since school started up again after spring break. Why?

Because of **Tommy** Mugersnot, who is the **meanest,** most terrible person in my **life.**

I thought I was finished with him, but he came back and he's up to his old rotten ways. Right before school ended last year, Mugersnot told everyone he was moving to Alaska to hang out with polar bears. I'm clueless about where he really went, because he never tells it the way it actually is. Aunt Gertie calls that "being loose with the truth."

If he really did go to Alaska, the land of **freezing** air, I wish he had **stayed** in his igloo.

3

Today at lunch, Mugersnot and his goons bombed me with open cartons of milk, soggy peanut butter sandwiches, and gooey bananas, and then they squirted my face with a bunch of ranch dressing packets. Just as I finished wiping off the gross stuff, another goon launched a Twinkie my way—but I ducked.

What really annoys me most about Mugersnot is the way he catches me in passing between classes or after school. That's when he and his goons shout,

"HEY, HEY, HEY! BEEP-BEEP-BEEP! IT'S ANDY JONES, THE WALKING COMPUTER, BEEP-BEEP-GEEEEEEEEK!"

At times like those, all I want to do is find the nearest sidewalk crack, slip into it, and disappear forever.

My war with Mugersnot began last year when I was a fifth grader. I took first place at school and beat him in the science fair. I was pretty shocked that I won, and Mugersnot was hopping mad about it. He jumped up and down and screamed, "It isn't fair!"

The way I see it, he's a poor loser. He even wrote a letter to the school newspaper saying the whole science fair was rigged in my favor. That's when the "BEEP-BEEP" thing started. Mugersnot didn't like that I could turn fractions into decimals on the large whiteboard in Mrs. Duncan's math class faster than anybody else. He told the kids at school that I was a computer, not a human, because nobody could multiply, divide, add, and subtract that fast.

4

I told Mugersnot, "It's pretty amazing what you can do if you practice your multiplication tables and stop wasting your time playing video games."

That's when he got really ticked and **shoved** his **knuckles** in my face.

$$\frac{x}{5} + 7 = -3$$
$$\frac{x}{5} + 7 - 7 = -3 - 7$$
$$\frac{x}{5} = 10$$
$$\frac{x}{5}(5) = -10\,(5)$$
$$x = 50$$

I thought my nose would be running with blood, but it wasn't. I was surprised when Mugersnot dropped his fists, turned, and walked away—but not before looking back at me and snarling, "You better watch yourself, Jones. I'm going to be your worst enemy." I knew he wasn't kidding.

Tuesday April 4
Hairy Mole

Today was the worst day of my life. After school, Mugersnot and his goons followed me to my locker. I tried to outrun them even though the slick floor made me feel like I was wearing slippers on an ice rink. Somehow I got to my locker before Mugersnot and quickly grabbed my books and backpack. Just when I was about to leave, I saw it. The hand with the hairy mole popping out like the bulging eye of a zombie. Mugersnot slammed my locker shut and sneered, "BEEP-BEEP-BEEP, going home, Andy Jones?"

Before long, his goons showed up and started chanting, "**BEEP... BEEP... BEEP... BEEEEEEEEEEEEEP!**" They opened their mouths wide and cackled with laughter. That's when I saw their scummy fanged teeth. Okay, I'm stretching the truth a little. Aunt Gertie always warns me, "Andy, don't stretch the truth. The seams will always pop." I think she means I'll be found out. So yeah, Mugersnot and his gang didn't have fanged teeth, but their teeth were scummy and their breath smelled like moldy cheese. That much is true.

What happened next surprised me because I'm not an "in-your-face" kind of kid. I got mad. I don't know where my brain went, but I clenched my fists, pulled one back, closed my eyes, and with all my strength I threw my best punch at Mugersnot.

I hit empty air.
I froze.

Mugersnot and his gang didn't let up.

Mugersnot and his goons shrieked with laughter. I yelled, "You're all a bunch of half-witted morons with subzero IQ," but my voice came out squeaking like a cornered mouse.

It was an awkward moment. I locked eyes with Mugersnot. He stared at me like a snake about to strike. I wasn't going to let him or his goons think they'd gotten to me. I puffed my chest like a Ninja Warrior and yelled, "LEAVE ME ALONE!"

Okay, I didn't really yell any of that. If my best friend Flynn had videoed the whole thing, anyone could have seen that I was only a nerdy wimp standing silent like super glue had just been smeared over my lips.

They continued jeering, "BEEP-BEEP-LOSER... BEEP-BEEP-LOSER!" Almost every kid leaving school heard them and came rushing to the scene like free video games were being given out. That's when I wanted to disappear and time-travel to another universe. I dropped my books and backpack and clapped my hands over my ears. I pushed past Mugersnot, the goons, and the swarm of kids, and I ran. The shouts of "BEEP-BEEP-LOSER" changed to "RUN ANDY RUN!"

When I got to my front yard, I collapsed on the grass, belly down, and stared at an earthworm inches from my nose. I picked him up and asked,

"Have you ever had the worst day of your life?"

7

Wednesday April 5
Pod of Whales

I'm glad I didn't have the second-worst day of my life today. When I got to school, I was called to the office to get my backpack and books. Mrs. Winchell, the school's secretary, gave me a polite smile and said, "Don't let it get to you!" Hearing that didn't make me feel any better.

Things started to get better during science when Mr. Bullard asked the class a question: "Which object, a heavy one or a light one, would fall faster if they were both dropped at the same time and from the same height?" I raised my hand and said, "The heavy one would fall faster, like blubber-boy Mugersnot."

The class laughed and even Prudence Glummer cracked a smile. Mugersnot kicked my desk chair. Mr. Bullard told me to "watch my words." Mugersnot growled, "Yeah, Andy, watch your words!" His hot breath almost left a scorch mark on my neck.

I raised my hand and asked Mr. Bullard if I could tell the class about Newton's third law of motion. I explained how every action always brings about an equal and opposite reaction. Then I gave the example that when I push Mugersnot's anger button, he kicks my chair.

Everyone laughed again until Mr. Bullard dropped a hammer and a feather on the metal table at the front of the room and said, "Atmosphere is the difference!" Then the class got quiet. Mr. Bullard started talking about how in 1971 an Apollo 15 astronaut went to the moon and dropped a hammer and a feather. He told the class that since there is no atmosphere on the moon, there was no resistance to either object; there was no air to slow down the lightweight feather more than the heavyweight hammer, so they both fell at the same speed and landed at the same time.

I wanted to know more, so I raised my hand. Mr. Bullard told me to keep my question "short and sweet." I asked, "What would happen if Mugersnot and me were the same weight and height, and we jumped off a fifty-foot cliff into a river together, but I jumped feet first, straight like an arrow, and Mugersnot jumped belly-down, flat like a mattress? Who would splash into the river first?"

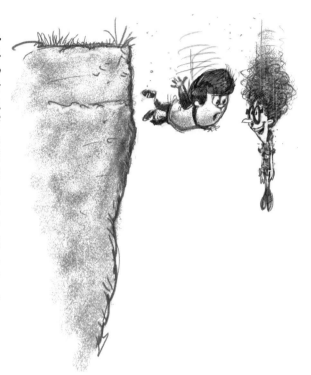

Mr. Bullard answered, "You would hit the water before the belly-down jumper because of his flat body position. He would have greater air resistance and aerodynamic drag." Everyone cracked up. I glanced over at Mugersnot.

His face could have been easily switched out for a red light.

Mr. Bullard got stern and told the class to settle down, but not before he gave me that look that said, "Enough, Andy." That's when he walked over to his desk, picked up a piece of paper, came over, and dropped it on top of my science book, letting me know that I have three days to get my application in to enter this year's science fair.

9

Mugersnot leaned over and whispered, "Jones, don't even think about taking first place again. It ain't gonna happen!"

Sure enough, Mugersnot is already doubling down his efforts to make my life at Woodside a nightmare. The bell rang and I ran out of class. Prudence smiled at me.

I wish it had been Suzy, the cute new cheerleader.

Thursday April 6

Duck and Dash

Mugersnot is on the move. He's not doubling down, he's tripling down on his efforts to mess with me. Three Twinkies and three milk bombs were lobbed my way at lunch. I dodged them all, even the one that was a dud.

After school, Mugersnot followed me to my locker without his brutes. When I put my last book in my backpack and turned to leave, Mugersnot shoved his face inches from mine. "What's up, science fact guy?" His breath was so bad it could have peeled the stickers off my locker. He slapped his hands on the wall above my head.

I was trapped by a **monster** that had sticker-peeling breath and rotten-egg-smelling **armpits.**

I thought I was going to suffocate, but then remembered a video Flynn showed me yesterday on his "random" YouTube channel called "Self-Defense for Wimps." The video taught a move called the "Duck and Dash." The goal is to distract your attacker any way you can and look for the first chance to duck under their armpit and dash away. Now, that move came to my rescue perfectly.

I aimed a swift kick to Mugersnot's right kneecap. I missed, but the kick startled him enough that he dropped his right arm and I was able to duck and dash under his other arm while yelling,

"Your armpits smell like rotting eggs!"

I ran home and called Flynn to tell him what had happened. He was glad his video had helped me. He asked if I had seen his other video, "Rolling." Flynn was stoked that it had gotten 543 views. It was a thirty-second clip of a gigantic trampoline rolling down a street and somehow avoiding hitting all the cars and kids in the area.

Flynn understands that what worries me most about Mugersnot is my fear of him turning into my forever bully. What can I do? Should I move to another planet? That won't work because, as far as I know, no one has ever built a house on one. But if someone does build space huts on Mars and starts a life-sustaining colony,

I'll be the first one on the rocket ship.

I've seriously considered changing schools, but that won't work for reasons I don't want to go into. Should I try and disguise myself by dying my hair blue or wearing a wig? No, that won't work because Aunt Gertie told me chemicals in hair dyes are toxic and you could have an allergic reaction where your face swells up like a soccer ball. And wigs won't work either, because they're itchy and hot. I wore a green one when I was in the school play and played the Jolly Green Giant.

I ended up **ditching** the wig when my **scalp** began to itch.

I thought for sure I had a serious case of head lice. As it turned out, I did. Aunt Gertie put some smelly stuff on my scalp to get rid of it.

Maybe I should make friends with the guys on the football team and let them be my bully busters! On second thought, maybe not... The football team has some of the basketball players on it, and when I tried to hang out with the basketball team last year before Mugersnot left for Alaska, it was a disaster. Those guys forced me to give them sticks of gum by twisting my arm until I gave in, and then they fleeced my pockets and had me turn over my gummy bears too.

13

Kung Fu Kick

I felt discouraged about my lousy plans to get Mugersnot off my back, so I called Flynn to see if he had a better idea. He said I should get smart on how to bust this bully and do two things:

1) Watch kung fu YouTube videos and put the moves into practice.
2) Super-charge my muscles by eating steak three times a week for dinner.

Flynn was sure that if I did these things I'd be ready to fight my battles with Mugersnot and land my punches and kicks. I told him it wouldn't work. Mom doesn't buy beef that often. She says it costs too much. Also—last year, I thought I could rock the world as a kung fu champ. But the only thing I rocked was my hamstring after I did a kung fu kick for the first time.

The **pain** was so bad that I couldn't walk without **hurting** for **6** months.

Besides, even if I did eat steak and watch kung fu videos, I can't build my courage that way. Courage begins on the inside, and I don't know how to make that happen. My guts are strong when I'm in math and science classes, but the rest of the time, when I face Mugersnot, those guts disappear. This I know: it will take a miracle for Mugersnot to evaporate and go away. If that happened, I'd be a new Andy, happily skipping rope, turning handstands, and popping a few wheelies (if I get my stolen bike back).

Getting the bully monster off my back would be such a relief that I'd also have a victory party and invite every nice person I know, even Mr. Smith, the postman. Pizza and ice cream would flow like Willy Wonka's river of chocolate.

Imagining my celebration just got me thinking about Flynn coming to the party and recording it and sharing it on his YouTube channel. The truth is, Flynn would run from the idea. Flynn's not a social guy, and he hates going to parties. But he might be interested in making a video of me talking to people at the mall about bully busting and asking them how to find a bully buster. The video could be Flynn's best work yet. He could get millions of views. He'd be a YouTube sensation!

I sure **hope** I'm not **dreaming** about this one.

Worst Dessert
in the World

Flynn just left my house. I invited him over for his favorite dessert, Aunt Gertie's apple pie with vanilla ice cream. I wanted him to be in a good mood so we could have an important discussion about making that video. It didn't work out the way I planned, though.

Things started going south when Aunt Gertie told me she couldn't make an apple pie because she'd run out of apples. Then she told me she would make rhubarb pie because she had plenty of it in her garden. That bummed me out. Rhubarb pie is the worst dessert in the world. Rhubarb is a vegetable that tastes like sour celery, but that doesn't stop Aunt Gertie from picking it, boiling it, and turning it into a pie that's meant to punish the eater. My little brother George has an iron kettle for a stomach, and he'll devour his slice without a problem. Flynn won't eat it because he's allergic to rhubarb.

If he **ate** it, he would end up with **swollen** lips.

Because we didn't have apples and since Flynn was allergic to rhubarb, the only dessert he got was a tiny bit of ice cream because George had almost finished off the carton. George says he's extra hungry coming home from school after stuffing his pockets full of grasshoppers. He collects them every day. He enjoys it as much as eating ice cream.

I really think that when **George** grows up, he's going to be a grasshopperologist.

I wasn't happy that Flynn barely got a spoonful, and I couldn't believe it when I heard him say thank you to Aunt Gertie for the ice cream and for baking the horrible pie. I wouldn't have done that. My best friend showed manners and grace. That's what Aunt Gertie calls it, at least. Later, Aunt Gertie told me to practice good manners like Flynn and to say please and thank you anytime anyone did something nice for me, whether or not it meets my expectations.

This I know: If Flynn could give grace to Aunt Gertie for making the worst dessert in the world and only having one spoonful of ice cream, then he should be able to give me some of that grace stuff too and be down for making my bully buster video.

When I told Flynn my idea, I made sure I gave him plenty of details about how it would work. I was hoping he would feel at least a tiny bit of excitement about it, but he didn't. He stared at me like a cow staring at a gate.

I didn't let his **bored** look
discourage me.

I ramped up my idea more, thinking that I could change his mind. I told him that he could throw in a cool song for background music, like "Eye of the Tiger" from the Rocky movie. Flynn didn't flinch. I tried harder. I told him that making the video was his moral duty and how it was as important as helping orphans in Africa. I went on and said, "Millions of bullied kids desperately need help to solve their bully problems! We can make a difference by coming up with a video that gives real survival tips on busting bullies and finding a bully buster." I closed by telling him,

"I could **become** the poster child of **bullying!**"

All Flynn said before he went home was, "Too bad Aunt Gertie didn't make the apple pie."

18

First Strike

I had a nightmare last night. Mugersnot threw a giant-sized Twinkie at my head, and I couldn't dodge it in time and got the worst splat of gooey white cream on my face. I was scared of seeing him at school today but he never showed up, which actually makes me even more scared. I'm worried about what his get-even scheme will be since I humiliated him in Mr. Bullard's class. Is he going to throw a dozen milk carton bombs my way at lunch or is he recruiting more kids to join his gang of goons? What if Mugersnot starts a cyberbullying campaign called "Attack of the Twinkies" and posts pictures online of me being pelted by hundreds of them?

Whatever nasty revenge plot Mugersnot is up to, it isn't going to stop me from coming up with my own list of first strike ideas... even if I never find the courage to carry them out.

First Strike ideas!
1. Squirt Superglue in Mugersnot's combination lock on his school locker.
2. Write a FAKE GUSHY letter from Mugersnot to Prudence Glummer.
3. Keep a stash of PINK Rubber erasers in my Backpack AND secretly pummel him whenever it's safe to do it.

The Only Gift

I couldn't sleep last night. I got up and grabbed my telescope and passed through the kitchen where Buckles, my four-footed friend, sleeps. His "Andy trackers" (that's what I call his ears) were on, so he woke up and joined me. We passed through the living room, where Mom was sleeping on the couch.

We got to the back door and stepped out into the yard. I set up the telescope that Mom gave me for Christmas. It was the only gift I liked. It wasn't hard deciding which one was best. My other gift was a pair of red polka-dotted socks from Aunt Gertie.

There isn't a day that goes by when Mom doesn't tell George and me how much she loves us. I don't know why, because we get on her nerves an awful lot. If I were to look up the word "patience" in the dictionary, I would see Mom's name next to it, and if I were to look up the word "perseverance" I would see her name next to that, too! Mom works really hard to keep it together for us. She has two and a half jobs. Her half job is crocheting potholders and selling them at the flea market on Saturday morning. Her day job is cleaning houses three to five days a week, and her evening job is working as an emergency dispatcher at the police station Monday to Friday from 3 p.m. to 11 p.m.

The only day she has **off** is **Sunday,** and she calls it her "**sleep catch-up day.**"

When Mom's working dispatch, Aunt Gertie comes over to stay with George and me and cooks us dinner (sometimes she burns it), and afterwards we usually play a video game for thirty minutes, but only after we spend thirty minutes reading something. George will read with Aunt Gertie. When our gaming time is up, she'll tell George and me to go to bed, but not before she makes us listen to one of her boring Texas stories.

One time she told us about how she and her sister Polly grew up in Amarillo, Texas. Aunt Gertie worked in a meat-packing plant, a place where cows don't have a happy ending. She loves telling George and me that "everything's bigger in Texas!" Another time she told us a story about a town that has the world's largest jackrabbit. It's an eight-foot-high rabbit sculpture built in 1962. It was made to attract people to the jackrabbit roping competition that happens somewhere in Texas. And another time,

Aunt Gertie told us a story about the world's **largest** **24**-foot-tall Dalmatian dog **fire** hydrant.

It is also somewhere in Texas and it weighs over 4,500 pounds and blasts 1,500 gallons of water every minute. I'd love to turn that on Mugersnot and his nasty brats.

Shaggy Dog

I hung out last night with Buckles and we did some amazing stargazing, looking up at the twinkly night-lights in the sky. I could tell Buckles thought those stars were pretty awesome too! He kept staring upwards and didn't move an inch. George calls Buckles a "shaggy dog," but the dog books tell me he's an Old English Sheepdog, one of those dog breeds that guard sheep. I'm sure he's not a pure bred, though. He's got a little something else mixed in him too. Buckles has more shag on him than our carpets. What I like best about the ol' boy is that he's huggable and fun! I think I've given him more hugs than I've given anybody in my family.

I wouldn't trade
Buckles
for anything.

Two years ago, I rescued him from the pound. When I first saw him, he was thin and smelled bad and his coat was oily like he had been sleeping under a car. The shelter guys found him eating banana peels from the garbage. Once I brought him home, he got a good scrubbing. I used Mom's strawberry shampoo and emptied the whole bottle on his back. A lot of water spilled out on the floor. Aunt Gertie wasn't thrilled about that.

She only got **over** it when Buckles went up to her, all dry and **sweet smelling**, and put one of his **paws** on her lap.

What I like most about Buckles is that he has *my* back. One time, when I was fishing, he started barking like crazy. I turned around and saw a four-foot-long timber rattler inching its way across the rock I was sitting on. I backed off fast and forgot about fishing any more that day.

Nothing Never Makes Something

Buckles and I went out again last night to do some more amazing gazing, but this time we went to the hill behind my backyard to get an even better view of the sky. I thought about how cool it would be to discover a new planet or cluster of stars. Mr. Bullard told our class that every star is a huge, hot ball of glowing gas and each of them creates their own light and energy. A star's gas comes from the thermonuclear fusion of hydrogen into helium, but my gas comes from Aunt Gertie's burritos after she stuffs them full of beans.

Before I set up my telescope, Buckles and I stretched back our necks and stared into the sky. I was feeling very "star struck" at the sight of so many stars splattered everywhere like sparkly glitter on black paper.

Looking at that **stunning** display,

I couldn't help but wonder about a few things. Why stars? How did they get here? Were they just random, cosmic explosions? Why don't they fall out of the sky? I looked over at Buckles. He sat like a statue, taking in the view. I didn't know what his questions were, but I figured he might have a few like mine. I told him that stars don't fall out of the sky because they're not little lights hanging around the Earth. Instead, they're so far away that Earth's gravity has no effect on them. The stars are like our sun with their own sets of planets around them. It's pretty crazy how celestial traffic is organized and how Earth appears to be in just the right place in our Milky Way galaxy. Mr. Bullard said that if the Earth were just a little closer to the sun, we would all be burnt toast.

Buckles barked. My dog is smart, so I asked him,

"Do you have any idea how many stars and galaxies are in the universe?"

He turned his head towards me as if to listen. I told him that on a clear night our eyes can see about five thousand stars, but there are hundreds of billions of stars that make up the Milky Way galaxy that we can't see.

Those star-watcher guys who use gigantic telescopes to get better views of space say there could be over ten trillion galaxies and planets spread all around the universe. If each galaxy is like ours with trillions of stars...

...then the total number of stars in the **universe** is a number with a whole lot of **zeros** behind it.

Buckles perked his ears up as I boggled his mind. I let him know that Earth is ninety-three million miles from the sun. The sun is so huge that over a million Earths could fit into it. The other planets in our solar system are perfectly placed; not one is too close or too far from the others. The Earth and moon are positioned just right for the water cycle and tides to work. If the Earth's orbit were a little bit farther from the sun, the oceans would freeze, and if it were a little bit closer, the oceans would boil and evaporate like water in a teapot.

"Maybe," I said to Buckles, "there really is an S.I.B.B.M.M.—that means a 'super-intelligent brilliant brain mastermind'—behind the incredible design in the universe, like a cosmic engineer."

Then I told Buckles something that confuses me. Whenever I read my science book during Mr. Bullard's class, it tells me that the order and design we see in the universe and in the world started out with a huge explosion, and it took a whole bunch of time working through some "random whatever" to get the universe organized and put together. That doesn't make a whole lot of sense, especially when Aunt Gertie tells me my room looks like a bomb exploded in it. She scolds me and says that I better get to work to clean it up. I sure wish that the "random whatever" would come along and pick up my Legos, make my bed, and hang up my clothes.

The chances of that happening are probably a trillion zillion to one.

The truth is, explosions don't make things come back together or make things look better.

They blow things up and never put stuff back. I remember the painful times when Aunt Gertie dragged George and me to a museum to "become cultured," as she says. I always felt relieved to get out of there, but also certain that an artist painted the paintings we saw. Paintings like those don't just explode into looking nice. I have to admit, though, some of the weirder paintings do look like an explosion happened on them. Aunt Gertie tells George and me that it's called "art."

The way I see it, you need someone with some sort of intelligence to make something look good. I mean, suppose I were to dump a bunch of rocks and magnets on a table and then just sit and wait for them to put my science project together for me. That would be crazy. I'm pretty sure that if I ever told Aunt Gertie that, she would say "my brains were falling out of my bucket." I don't have to be a rocket scientist to know this: Nothing never makes something.

I wish it worked that way, though, because that would be awesome! I could lie back in George's hammock and expect "nothing" to bring me a first-place ribbon at the science fair.

I glanced over at Buckles, who was shaking his head up and down. He looked like he was agreeing, but he also could have just had a mosquito buzzing around his ear. When I was finally done talking, Buckles yawned wide. It wasn't because he was bored. In dog language, a yawn meant he was enjoying himself. At least, that's what Wikipedia told me.

Dreams and Ice Cream

I was listening to Mr. Bullard in class today. He told us that the universe has a definite beginning point, and that Albert Einstein, the great physicist, said so. Mr. Bullard brought out a balloon, blew air into it, and held it up. Then he talked about how the universe is like an expanding balloon, stretching bigger and bigger and bigger. He took some steps back, released the balloon's air, and said when this happens,

the **universe** becomes smaller and **smaller** until it finally **collapses** to its starting point.

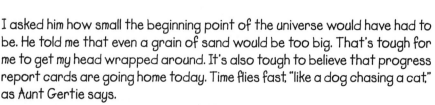

I asked him how small the beginning point of the universe would have had to be. He told me that even a grain of sand would be too big. That's tough for me to get my head wrapped around. It's also tough to believe that progress report cards are going home today. Time flies fast, "like a dog chasing a cat," as Aunt Gertie says.

I was super tired when I came home from school and slept until dinner. I had a funny dream. It didn't make me laugh, but it made me think. My dream had Professor Hubble in it. This guy was an old dude who has a huge telescope named after him, called the Hubble Space Telescope. I dreamed Professor Hubble pulled a rubber band and black marker from his pocket. The next thing he did was mark tiny dots on the rubber band. Then he stretched it out. I watched carefully and saw how the black dots moved farther away from each other as the band stretched. That's when I got it. The rubber band is supposed to be the universe expanding just like the balloon filling up with air, and the black dots are supposed to be galaxies in the universe. Professor Hubble said the spinning galaxies move away from each other as the universe expands and gets bigger.

Just when I was about to ask Professor Hubble a question in my dream, I heard my name called.

"Andy!"

It was Mom. I wondered why she was not at work.

"Wake up! I'm taking you and George out for ice cream!" She doesn't usually take us out for special treats. We don't have extra money to spend on that kind of thing. But Mom told me the boss gave her the night off, and a lady from work gave her a twenty-dollar bill. The lady told Mom to get her boys a treat. I couldn't think of a better idea! That's a sweet lady!

We drove to Doodle Dud's Creamery to celebrate George and me getting a couple of A's on our progress report cards and to reward us for eating our vegetables. The last part is half a lie though. The truth is, I always eat my vegetables but George doesn't. He's a master at hiding them in his napkin.

He **spits** his peas into it, bunches it up, and **throws** it away.

I ate the biggest banana split of my life tonight. George claims he ate the "biggest banana split in the world." It was far from it, though. It was just a junior scoop of ice cream, a few banana slices, and a small spoonful of fudge. I was having fun goofing around and stuck a piece of black licorice onto my front tooth. I pretended I'd knocked it out and fell to the floor in fake pain. George thought I had really done it, but Mom knew I was pulling a fast one. George only calmed down after I told him the truth. Then Mom told us a few jokes while George and I finished our splits.

"Boys, why do ducks have flat feet? To stamp out forest fires... Why do elephants have flat feet? To stamp out burning ducks... What did one eye say to the other eye? Don't look now, but something between us smells."

George **laughed** a lot but I didn't think Mom's **jokes** were funny.

31

After her last joke, Mom got serious. She started telling us how we should be packing our brains with knowledge about lots of things. She talked about the value of wisdom and making good decisions and positive choices that help yourself and others.

"Boys, there's more to life than just you; learn to be wise and don't waste time!"

Aunt Gertie is always telling us, "There are two things you can spend in life, money and time. Don't squander 'em, and don't forget, one of 'em you never get back." George always says "money" and I always say "time." I'm right.

Then Mom reminded George and me not to be afraid to struggle to understand, because that's how we learn. That's what smart people do. They keep asking questions until they don't have as much fuzziness in their brain. Mom wants George and me to read lots of different kinds of books and stop wasting our "one and only life" playing video games or staring at the "dumb screen," which is her name for TV. Mom believes looking at screens for too long turns you into a mashed potato head, or someone who has soft and mushy brains because they don't like to learn. Mom tells us that the more we watch the dumb screen, the bigger our mashed potato head will get and the less we'll want to understand new things and grow.

I'm not sure what she means by "grow." I'm not a plant.

32

After I took my last bite of ice cream, Mom quoted Albert Einstein: "'The measure of intelligence is the ability to change.'" She told us that Einstein had the brainpower of a hundred rocket scientists.

Mom must really like this guy's thinking, because last night she gave us another quote from him.

"Remember, Andy and George, what Einstein said:

'Life is like riding a bicycle. To keep your balance, you keep moving.'

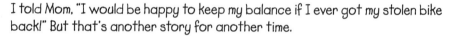

I told Mom, "I would be happy to keep my balance if I ever got my stolen bike back!" But that's another story for another time.

I have to say Mom is one of the nicest people you could ever talk to. You might get to hear her voice if you call 911, but I hope you never have to. Every night, she gets calls from lots of people. One time, she got a call from a panicked kid who almost burned his whole house down after deciding he wanted to roast marshmallows in his bedroom. The kid stacked wooden blocks to make a campfire and used pick-up sticks to put the marshmallows on. He got a hold of matches and tried lighting the wood, but the only things that caught fire were the curtains in his room. Everyone made it out of the house, except the goldfish. But it lived in water, so it was okay.

I respect Mom a lot. She works hard and doesn't give up. She's the one in our family who, as Aunt Gertie says, "milks the cow and creams the butter." Dad skipped out after George was born and I was six, so Mom pretty much always took care of us on her own. I don't know much about Dad because, when he lived with us, he was never around. Mom will tell us the story one day.

Nasty Note

Mugersnot passed a nasty note about me in Mr. Bullard's class today. I only found out about it because Prudence Glummer showed me. He drew a picture of me standing next to a science project called, "Which toilet flushes Andy's poops the best?" Prudence said not to worry because she got the note before anyone else saw it.

I sure hope he doesn't post anything like that online.

Hundred-Pound Weight

I **woke** up with a hundred-pound weight **licking** my face. It was Buckles.

I didn't mind. It's nice to have someone like you that much. Buckles put his head on my stomach, and I rubbed his back and asked him, "Could there really be an awesome Someone who thought you up and put all your different pieces together, like what I do when I'm making a robot out of Legos? I wonder if that Someone came up with all the people and other living things out there too?"

Buckles flipped over onto his back, curled his paws, and yawned wide. I could tell he was looking for a good belly scratch. I gave him one and then asked him another question. "What if that Someone put all the hundreds of trillions of stars, planets, and galaxies in their places and had a whole lot of fun doing it?"

Buckles rolled over onto his belly and spread out his pudgy legs flat behind him. They reminded me of fat pork chops. He looked into my eyes and gave me a smirky grin, rolled his lips back, and showed off his tiny, crooked bottom teeth. Maybe he knows something I don't.

Sunday April 16
Awful Driver

I've only been to church once. I don't miss it because I didn't understand what the preacher was talking about that one time. Mom doesn't go because it's the only day of the week she can sleep late. Aunt Gertie offers to take George and me to church in her 1965 Ford Thunderbird, but we won't go because she's an awful driver. George and I made a pact to never get into Aunt Gertie's old T again as long as she's doing the driving. The times we rode with her were like riding in a roller coaster that had gone off its tracks.

If there's one thing I know, it's that Aunt Gertie's Thunderbird has more dents than George and I can count. She tells us she's never getting the old T smoothed out because dents give it "character." Then she tells us how "every dent tells a story!"

I can't forget the time when George and I rode with her to the dollar store. We didn't make it because she rammed into a curb trying to turn right while blowing past a stop sign. Aunt Gertie said it happened because she lost control after accidentally pressing down on the accelerator, and doing that sent the old T airborne for a second or two until it came down hard on the pavement. We bounced around like a gigantic rubber ball and only stopped after hitting a fire hydrant and making a fifty-foot gusher spring up. A small crowd watched our crazy show from across the street, and it was a good thing someone called the fire department because the gusher seemed to grow and grow. Those guys arrived quickly and turned off the valve so the gusher turned into a trickle.

After all that, George and I slunk even lower in our seats because we didn't want anyone from school or our neighborhood to see us. But Aunt Gertie didn't mind being a big deal. She never has. She hopped out of the old T and started waving to the folks standing around, like she expected them to want her autograph or something. She told George and me to relax, and right then the police officers showed up. George got nervous and scared, and he kept asking them if we were going to jail. I laughed and said,

"**No!** They only wanted us to **step out** of the car to answer a few questions."

One of the officers told us we were "Dang lucky no one got hurt." I said, "It wasn't luck, the angels get the credit." That's what Aunt Gertie is always telling us. "Boys, don't worry, the Heavenly King has His Heavenly Squad watching our every move."

After that embarrassing ordeal, George and I should have learned our lesson to never ride in the old T when Aunt Gertie's behind the wheel.

But we didn't.

We for sure learned it a couple of weeks later when she invited us to come with her to church. George and I only went because she promised us that we would go out to our favorite restaurant afterwards, Flipping Jacks, where we could chow down on pancakes. With stacks of pancakes on our minds, George and I hopped into the old T. As soon as we were buckled in, Aunt Gertie started chatting on her cell phone, and right away I politely told her that wasn't a good idea. She didn't listen to me and instead continued talking until she accidentally dropped her phone.

Instead of LEAVING IT ON THE FLOOR OF THE CAR, Aunt Gertie reached down to pick it up, taking her eyes off the road, and slammed into a parked car on our right side. I was glad the Heavenly Squad watched out for us, because nobody got a scratch or a bruise. The other car sure got an ugly makeover, though. Aunt Gertie left a note on the car's cracked windshield, saying how sorry she was and that she would pay for the repairs. I thought she should have offered the owner a new car. After we drove away, Aunt Gertie brushed everything off, saying, "I guess the enemy doesn't want us to get to church." I wasn't sure what enemy she was talking about. Once we got to church and walked in and sat down, a lady with a beehive hairdo stood up front and started going on about a rummage sale. I thought Mom should sell her potholders there.

After the lady was done, everyone started singing about grace being amazing, and when that was over the preacher started his sermon. I took out one of the short pencils from the back of the pew and doodled on the program.

I made the preacher look like the Terminator but gave him the name "the Sermonator."

I was having too much fun, and it stopped when Aunt Gertie gave me her stink eye, which meant I better stop and listen to the preacher. I had a hard time with that because his voice sounded like a church steeple had gotten stuck in his throat.

He stretched every word so each one sounded long and flat. "JEEEEEEZUS izzzz thuuuuuuu gooooood Shepheeeeeerd." I nodded my head, happily sleeping through it until Aunt Gertie elbowed me. I jerked awake and looked over at George. He was fiddling with a small grasshopper.

I guess he'd **pulled** it out from his shirt pocket. I don't know why he wasn't elbowed.

I don't know much about the Bible except that the main guy in it is Jesus. From what I've heard about him, he was a carpenter who did some weird but cool stuff like changing water into wine and making a small kid's lunch feed five thousand people. It doesn't sound like he was a boring religious dude. Aunt Gertie says Jesus hung out with broken, messy people. He fixed up the losers and later called them friends. Aunt Gertie tells me to follow Jesus' words about doing to others like you want them to do to you. I guess that means you better be nice to people and treat them right. I could never be "nice" to Mugersnot though, because...

...he's the **worst** bully in the universe.

Runniest Eggs

I ate one of Mom's runniest eggs ever for breakfast today. I asked her if I could have a straw instead of a fork to get it down.

She didn't think that was **funny** and gave me a **stern** look.

I told her the egg looked like gooey snail slime and it was impossible for me to eat it. Mom lectured me about the importance of being grateful, saying, "Gratitude is the attitude." Then she piled on some guilt and reminded me that I could be an orphan living in India dying of hunger. That's when I snapped back and said, "I would be more than thrilled to feed the orphan my egg. How should I send it?"

Mom wasn't happy with that answer either, so she sent me to my room and told me to write a hundred times on a piece of paper, "I will not be ungrateful and smart-mouthed to Mom." It took me almost an hour to finish writing it. When I was done, I put together a large Lego wall. After I put the last piece on, Mom walked into my room with Buckles on her heels. The old boy rushed me and crashed into my wall on the way, breaking it into a billion pieces. I wasn't too mad because Buckles is such a great dog and never gets into trouble—except for the time he put a couple of dog bones under Mom's pillow.

41

Mom said my Lego wall was designed well.

Then she asked me about my science fair project. I told her I probably wasn't going to do one. That's when her jaw dropped. She was so proud that I won last year and thought I was for sure going to do another one. I can't tell her the real reason I don't want to enter this year. If I tell her what goes on at school with Mugersnot, she'll get worried and get what Aunt Gertie calls a "worry wrinkle."

Mom felt better when I told her that, if I did enter the science fair, I'd make a model of a super cool colony on Mars and make some space dome huts that would connect to each other through tubes. My colony would have a high wall around it, protecting it from wind, sandstorms, and space invaders.

After the words "space invaders" left my mouth, Mom told me terrible news. Her youngest brother is coming to visit, and he's sleeping on the bottom bunk of my bed.

I'm annoyed that my space is going to be invaded and no one asked me what I would think about it. It's too bad that he can't stay with George, but he sleeps in a hammock on the back porch that Mom and Aunt Gertie closed up last year.

What I know so far is that Mom's brother is going to be doing some kind of special research. This I am sure of:

I AM NOT LOOKING FORWARD TO A RESEARCH MOLE SPACE INVADER INVADING MY ROOM.

AAAAAAAAAAAAAAGHHHH!!!!

I'm also sure that the Space Invader will tell more crazy Texas stories like Aunt Gertie, plus he'll likely be keeping me awake all night with awful snoring, or as Aunt Gertie puts it, "callin' the hogs."

Tuesday April 18

Tongue Taming

I was walking down the hall, minding my own business, when Mugersnot stuck his foot out to trip me. I would have done a serious face-plant if Flynn hadn't caught my arm. I don't know what to do about Mugersnot. I'm not happy that I still don't have a bully busting plan or some kind of bully buster helping me out. If only Flynn would make my video, then my bully problems would be solved.

School let out early today. It was nice to see Mom at home. She was baking chocolate chip cookies before she left for work. After downing a half dozen, I told Mom how unhappy I was about the Space Invader's visit. She scolded me and said, "Andy, stop being selfish! You'll learn from the experience." "I won't live long enough to do that," is what I wanted to say. But I didn't. Being sent to my room by an annoyed Mom is not the way I want to spend my afternoon, especially since I want to try and hook a fish later on.

Aunt Gertie is always saying that the only control I get in life is self-control, so I better get into the habit of "tongue taming," as she calls it. She also says it took me two years to learn to "flap my gums" and talk, but it's going to take the rest of my life for me to learn how to tame my tongue.

It's a "wild **bucking** bronco" in Aunt Gertie's dictionary.

I'm dreading the Space Invader's visit almost as much as Mugersnot throwing a dozen milk bombs at me. Mom's trying to cheer me up by doing her best to convince me how awesome her brother is. She'll say, "Andy, there's no one as brainy and nice as your uncle."

I doubt that. Mom also tells me the Space Invader was a lot like me while he was growing up. I doubt that too.

I was heading out the door with my fishing pole with Buckles at my side, when Mom cornered me and talked more about the Space Invader. She went on about how interesting and wonderful his job is and how he's a published author, lecturer, and world traveler and that Israel is one of his favorite places to visit. I told her, "Cool," with as much enthusiasm as I would give a plate of boiled Brussels sprouts.

Then I let my "bucking bronco" out of the gate and snapped, "Mom, give me a break, can work ever be interesting and wonderful? I'm not throwing a party shoveling snow." Mom raised her eyebrows and looked at me like she was about to ground me. But she didn't. I got grace.

Instead, she sweetly said, "Andy, imagine this: You're lying bored in a hospital bed with two broken legs and two broken arms and you're tied up in traction, and you've been like that for over a week. Wouldn't you be thrilled if you were suddenly healed and you could leap out of your bed with two strong legs and arms that could shovel snow?"

It was a good thing I remembered to tame my tongue because I almost bucked and said, "Not if I could lie back, watch cartoons, and eat donuts and Pop-Tarts."

Raiders of the Lost Ark and Pop-Tarts

I told Mom I didn't want to go to school because I woke up with a stomachache, but the truth is, I'm still super stressed about the Space Invader taking over my room. Since Mom was home from work this morning, she said I could stay home if I did all my chores and read for three hours. Reading and doing chores is a lot better than being at school and dodging Mugersnot's Twinkie attacks. I would cheerfully do chores—even George's—for a year, if Mom canceled the Space Invader's visit.

Mom poured me a cup of ginger tea that smelled like rotting potatoes. She said I had to drink it because it would help my stomach feel better. I told her only a Pop-Tart would do that. I kept asking her for one, and she kept saying, "Not now." Mom sat down at the table with me, drinking the same rotting potato tea, to tell me more about the Space Invader. I wanted to make a fast dash to the bathroom, but I thought there might be a chance she'd give me a Pop-Tart if I sat quietly and listened to her.

I did my best to look **interested** in everything Mom was **talking** about,...

...especially the part when she described what the Space Invader was like when he was a kid. She said he loved dirt and dug a lot of holes in their backyard, and that's why they started spelling his name D-u-g instead of

47

D-o-u-g. Then Mom asked me to guess what the Space Invader's job was. I guessed ditch digger. She gave me a "you've got to be kidding!" look and told me he was an archaeologist.

I let her know that I **already** knew all about those guys because I'd seen the **Indiana Jones** movies.

That was the wrong thing to say, because for the next hour I got an information dump. Mom didn't want me to have the Hollywood idea of what archaeologists do.

When she was done talking, I couldn't help but think that she should have been an archaeologist too, because she's stoked about archaeology and knows a lot of stuff about it. Mom asked me if I had learned anything from what she told me. "Sure," I said quickly. "Archaeologists dig around in the dirt and get pumped about discovering crusty pots, clay bowls, dinosaur bones, stone tools, and dusty manuscripts." Mom smiled when I admitted that the Space Invader does have a pretty cool job since he plays in the dirt and gets paid for it!

Then I asked her the most important question: "Can I have a Pop-Tart?"

She didn't **think** I was a very **good** listener.

Curiosity Rover

A couple of nights ago, I dreamed about discovering a lost colony on Mars, built by a Martian civilization that constructed a high wall to protect themselves from space invaders. I was in charge of rebuilding the ruined walls of their city. I'm not sure why I had this dream...

...**maybe** it was because of seeing Flynn's **Mars** photo the other day.

The photo Flynn showed me was taken by NASA's Curiosity Rover, a car-sized robotic rover that goes around taking pictures on Mars. The Rover had taken a picture of something that Flynn said was the ruins of a walled city on Mars. Flynn thought it was evidence of a lost Martian civilization and the photo was proof that intelligent creatures once lived there. I told him that it proved nothing, and the photo was staged or altered by someone good at Photoshop. He didn't agree. But even if the photo is fake, I guess it's cool to imagine the possibility that there might have been a colony once living on the Red Planet. The more I think about it, the more I like the idea of building a Mars civilization for my science project and figuring out whether or not human life can successfully live there.

49

Friday
April 21
Snooping

I'm glad dinner is over. Aunt Gertie made meatballs tonight. She always puts a funky spice or two in them that smells like my sweaty gym socks. There isn't a day that goes by when Mom or Aunt Gertie doesn't tell George and me to be thankful that we have something to eat, even if it tastes nasty.

I wanted to do a somersault at lunch because Mugersnot didn't show up again today, which meant no dodging Twinkies, milk bombs, or his goons.

That's what I'm **thankful** for!

After school, I turned in my entry form for the science fair. Mr. Bullard was happy. Mom was happy. Aunt Gertie was happy. Mugersnot won't be happy. He'll be miffed when he hears that I'm entering again this year. But that's his problem. I've got plenty of problems to solve in figuring out a way to keep the oxygen, water, and food flowing on Mars and designing some kind of a protective wall around the colony so space invaders can't break in.

Mr. Bullard liked my ideas for my project. He said I need to get busy because the science fair is coming soon. He asked me about last year's fair and what I liked best. He gave me a funny look when I told him it was the donuts Miss Diddle brought in for everyone who entered a project.

I must have **downed** at least five **jelly-filled** ones.

I saw Mugersnot's science project entry form on Mr. Bullard's desk. It was right on top of his paper pile. I couldn't read what Mugersnot's project was because his handwriting was loose and sloppy. He must have been writing with his toes. Someone should get Mugersnot a journal so he can leave his scribbling behind. I'm not getting him one, because I don't do nice to bullies, especially the worst bully in the universe.

Yesterday, Aunt Gertie told me my journal had fallen on the floor and landed wide open! She said she couldn't help but notice how my handwriting has gotten a lot better. I'm not happy that she was snooping around and reading it, though. Journals don't open themselves up. I'm pretty sure she read a lot of what I wrote...

...and I can't help think she **saw** the part about her being an **awful** driver.

When I was washing dishes tonight, she asked me if I thought she was an awful driver. I had to speak the truth and told her, "YES!" What Aunt Gertie said next almost made me drop the cup I was drying. "I'm taking driving lessons." Then she asked if George and I would ride in the old T with her again when she was finished with the class.

I told her, "Maybe, but I can't speak for George."

Counting the Hours

The Space Invader arrives in one week. I'm counting the hours until he's out the door and gone. If he lasts for two weeks, it will be 336 hours that he's here until he packs his bags and disappears.

I'm bracing for impact and preparing for the worst. Yesterday, Mom bought me earplugs. I'm plugging my ears so I don't have to hear the Space Invader's hog-calling.

I need my zzzzzzzzzzzzZZZ's.

Raccoon Eyes

Mugersnot was at school today, but he looked more like a raccoon than a kid. His eyes were rimmed with black circles and he looked like he hadn't slept for a month. He was probably up all weekend playing video games and tormenting other kids.

Looking like a **raccoon** didn't stop Mugersnot from **food-bombing** me at lunch.

I dodged his peanut butter and jelly sandwich but was hit on the back of my shirt and neck with a plastic cup of ranch dressing tossed by one of his nasty grenade goons.

Anyone who **saw** me would think I had been **bombed** by a large **bird dropping.**

Flynn felt bad for me and wiped it off with a napkin from his lunch sack, but he couldn't wipe away the ranch dressing smell.

I wasn't happy that I smelled like a tossed salad walking into Mr. Bullard's class. Mugersnot snickered and asked me if I wanted any croutons. There must be Somebody up there who is watching out for me, because the office called and Mugersnot had to leave the room, and he never came back to the class.

After I got home later, I couldn't stop thinking about what happened at lunch. I called Flynn and said, "Poke me with a fork, I AM DONE! I'm done letting Mugersnot use me as a bull's-eye!" Flynn didn't say anything except that he could now beat me in chess.

I didn't care about that, but I did care about coming up with an emergency survival plan.

EMERGENCY SURVIVAL PLAN

1. Sit with the squirrels in the far corner of the field at lunch. I'll be safely tucked away and not easily visible to anyone. Better to be alone than get food-bombed.

2. Never show up at my locker after school.

3. Carry out one of my get-even schemes. Like putting glue in Mugersnot's combination lock or pummeling him with erasers when he can't see me or writing a fake love letter to him from Prudence Glummer.

Tuesday April 25

Smirk and Snot and Checkmate

I did what I didn't want to do. I broke Rule #2 of my emergency survival plan: I went to my locker after school. There was no way around it; I needed my jacket and house key. Smirking Mugersnot was already standing there with folded arms.

He **blocked** me from getting to my locker. I would have rather had a large **brick wall** in my way.

I almost turned around to leave, but for a weird, unknown reason, I stood my ground. Maybe I was thinking I could blow out some serious gas, leaving his eyes burning with toxic fumes, that same stuff that comes out after I eat Aunt Gertie's burritos. But no gas was stirring in my gut, so that didn't happen. But what happened next was better, because I couldn't be blamed for it.

Mugersnot suddenly had a sneezing attack. Then he started coughing. His eyes watered and he doubled over, hacking like he was losing a lung. He moved away from my locker and I moved in with lightning speed, opened it,

55

grabbed my coat, and ran. I don't know why I looked back at Mugersnot, but I did. We locked eyes. Mugersnot yelled like a broken foghorn, "Your lame science project is going down!"

I turned around and kept running. Aunt Gertie would have been proud because I tamed my bucking bronco. What I wanted to yell back at Mugersnot was,

"IF ALL YOUR SCIENCE BRAINS WERE INK, YOU COULDN'T DOT AN I!"

I caught up with Flynn on my way home and told him what happened. All he said was his usual, "Ignore the bully!" I got a little mad and said, "I can't ignore ranch dressing on my neck, or keep dodging milk and Twinkie bombs, or hearing snotty words, or smelling Mugersnot's stinky armpits and toxic breath." I was ramping up, beginning to feel like I might be the worst-bullied kid ever (I know that's not true). Besides all of this ugly stuff, I also let Flynn know that it's no fun dealing with Mugersnot's nasty threats to destroy my science project.

Flynn didn't say anything about my rant. We walked the rest of the way home in silence. I think we both knew we had enough words between us. Once we got to my house, I went to the pantry and brought out a box of Cheezebitzies. We sat down at the table and devoured the whole box. I cracked a few jokes, like "What do you call an old snowman? Water!... How do you catch a whole school of fish? With bookworms!"

I wanted Flynn to be in a **lighter** mood so I could bring up my **Bully Buster** video idea.

When I finally did, Flynn nearly choked on the sip of water he was taking. When he was done coughing, he said, "*NO!*" So I said, "Why not?"

That's when he told me he hates going into places like malls and videotaping people as much as he hates eating rhubarb pie. He's allergic to the scene and breaks out in hives.

I figured it would take nothing short of a miracle for Flynn to make my bully busting video. I knew approaching him again about the idea was a dead-end road, so I challenged him to a game of chess instead. I put his king in check, and finished him off in two moves! "CHECKMATE!"

I **wish** it was that **easy** with Mugersnot.

Real Bummer

Flynn called after dinner and asked if I could give him a few tips on how to up his chess game. I told him I would, if he could get over his phobias and make the video. He told me he didn't want my chess moves that bad.

I wonder if I'll ever get the worst bully in the universe off my back. I also wonder if I'll ever get my ten-speed Huffy bike back. It was a real bummer when it was stolen on my birthday three months, two weeks, thirteen days, and twenty-three hours ago. Six hooded thugs wearing ski masks ran off with it. I'd only left it on the driveway for a minute to run into the house.

After I came out, I saw the thugs dashing down the street carrying my wheels. I chased them for several blocks, but they had a getaway plan. A pickup truck was waiting, and in a second they had thrown my bike into the back of it and sped away.

My bike had been a gift from Mom, and I'm pretty sure she had to sell a lot of potholders to pay for it. Now, I'm saving up for a new one. If I can wash enough cars at five bucks a pop, I'll reach my goal in three years. So far, I've washed one car, Aunt Gertie's Thunderbird. I scrubbed the old T until I could see my face in the chrome bumpers. While washing it, I counted thirty-nine dents, nine scratches, and three cracks on the windshield.

I was trying my best to get a dried-up bird dropping off the old T's back trunk...

...when Aunt Gertie came alongside me and put her hand on my shoulder. I think she wanted me to feel better by using some of that empathy stuff Mom says I should have more of. Aunt Gertie told me how bad she felt about my new bike being stolen the same day I got it (on my birthday) and how I could wash her car every week until I had enough money to buy a new bike. Then she tried to cheer me up by saying, "Whoever the lowlifes are that jacked your bike, they are so low that you couldn't put a rug under 'em!"

Hearing that didn't make me feel any better.

Mangled Metal Mess

I liked watching the squirrels today. I'm doing my best to keep up with my emergency survival plan, and so far the only rule I've kept is eating on the field at lunch. The only good thing about being out there...

...is making **friends** with the **squirrels** by tossing them a few peanuts.

I rode my scooter to school this morning, which has almost as many dents as Aunt Gertie's old T. Once I parked it in the bike rack, I couldn't help but notice the five monster-sized bikes next to it: the Mongoose Muncher, the Dynamo Star, the Huffington Hair-Raiser, the Strident Steeler, and the Stealth Hurricane.

60

I started to wish that they were mine. I just knew that those bikes would be in my dreams that night. Aunt Gertie calls that envy. Her words popped into my head: "Don't envy. It always puts a kink in your hose and stops up the good flow from a grateful heart." Mom tells me to be grateful and happy for what I have, but I don't do that very well.

After I parked my scooter, I picked up my backpack and started to walk away. That's when a strong gust of wind kicked up a small cyclone of leaves and dirt. I stopped to watch the action and noticed the little cyclone was heading towards the bike stand. It first hit my scooter. Then it hit the Mongoose Muncher, and that big bike teetered and fell hard, smacking down the Dynamo Star. The rest of the bikes toppled onto each other like brick dominos. It was the last bike, the Stealth Hurricane, that crashed the hardest—down it went like a lead ball on the cement. I cringed and covered my ears but kept my eyes wide open. What I saw was a mangled metal mess of spinning wheels and loose chains.

I was **shocked** that my scruffy **scooter** stood straight and tall, not having **budged** an inch.

During science class, I overheard Mugersnot moan about a "jerk" who had knocked over all the bikes in the bike rack and how his new Stealth Hurricane was messed up. I put my head down, trying hard not to smile.

Godzilla Pepper

I couldn't be happier. I'm going to have one more night of sleep without a hog-caller keeping me awake. Mom told me the Space Invader will be arriving early tomorrow evening. He is flying in from Israel.

I wasn't sure where Israel was, so I found it on a map. From where I'm at in Great Barrington, Massachusetts, Israel is 6,744 miles away across the Atlantic Ocean. Israel is a tiny country (about as big as New Jersey). It's in the Middle East and it's surrounded by some bigger countries like Jordan, Egypt, and Syria. After doing a little reading about Israel,

I really can't **figure** out why **just** about every **country** around them wants their **tiny** neighbor's land.

Israel is interesting. They've got the Sea of Galilee (which isn't a sea at all, it's a lake!) and the strange Dead Sea that is one-third salt. This much I know: nothing lives in that much salt. The only cool thing about the Dead Sea is that anyone can float in it—even Mugersnot.

I found a few more weird facts about Israel.

Weird Fact #1

Israelis eat the third-largest amount of vegetables and sweets of any country in the world. Mom's always telling George and me to eat our vegetables to knock out our sweet tooth.

Weird Fact #2

The world's largest Godzilla pepper was grown in Israel. It was recorded by the Guinness Book of World Records in 2013. The pepper was green and weighed more than a pound. I'll bet Aunt Gertie would love to put that in one of her burritos.

Weird Fact #3

An Israeli company came up with the world's first jellyfish repellent. Why don't they come up with the world's first bully repellent?

You Are Not Welcome,
Space Invader

After I ate my last bite of macaroni and cheese, the doorbell rang. Mom answered it, looking flustered, and said, "He's here!" She took the night off from work because she wanted to be around when the Space Invader showed up. Aunt Gertie didn't care about seeing him because she was invited to play poker with her girlfriends. She said, "There'll be plenty of visiting time later on."

Mom opened the door, and there he was, the Space Invader.

I have to admit I wasn't underwhelmed. He stood tall, wearing a ten-gallon cowboy hat, leather cowboy boots, and khaki green cargo pants with lots of pockets that George would love putting his grasshoppers in.

64

The *Space Invader* shredded my expectations.

I imagined him **short** like Aunt Gertie and Mom, who are **barely** five-foot-two.

I thought for sure I'd be meeting a small, grumpy, research mole with a greasy goatee wearing thick, black-rimmed glasses.

Instead, the Space Invader had a belly-warming smile that made me feel like I had already known him for a long time, even though Mom said I hadn't seen him since I was two. She hugged him tight like it had been a hundred years since they'd seen each other. I was definitely not going to be doing any of that hugging action. When the Space Invader came around to where I was sitting at the table, he stretched out his arm to shake my hand. His handshake was strong and firm, like a ditch digger's might be. He said how nice it was that he was seeing me again after so many years. I didn't think it was so nice.

He asked about George just as George ran into the room and shoved a grasshopper in the Space Invader's face.

I was surprised that the Space Invader laughed and told George how grasshoppers have ears on their bellies and smell with their antennas. George said he hadn't heard about that. The Space Invader also told George that in ancient times in Egypt, people ate grasshoppers, and when there was a good rainy year and plenty of grass to eat, they multiplied. He told us how, when there are tons of grasshoppers in one location, they'll change or morph into bigger versions of themselves and start swarming and eating everything in their path! That's when grasshoppers become locusts! Sometimes, those little dudes are not the farmers' friends, because they'll eat all of their crops.

The Space Invader was full of interesting facts, and I was beginning to think that he wasn't so bad after all. I was convinced when he opened his huge satchel, rummaged around, and brought out a small wrapped package. He slowly opened it, and in the middle of a wad of tissues were...

...two big dinosaur teeth!

I asked if the teeth were from a Tyrannosaurus Rex. He told me I was right, and I was smart for knowing that. I didn't tell him it was just a guess. The Space Invader placed a tooth in each of our hands and asked us if we would like to go on an archaeological dig to the South Dakota Badlands to excavate dinosaur bones. George got so excited he wanted to start packing his bag right away. The Space Invader told him to "slow his roll" because we wouldn't go until next year.

Maybe having the Space Invader around isn't such a bad idea. He does seem to know about a lot of things. He asked George and me cool questions like, "If you could be invisible for a day, what would you do?" and "If you could make one rule, what would it be?" and "If you could invent something, what would it be?" George and I couldn't stop talking about our answers. Mom left the room and came back with mugs of hot chocolate. Believe me, it tastes a million times better than her rotten-potato-smelling tea. I guzzled it down right away because Mom doesn't make it too hot. After I drank the last drop,

I stuck my **finger** in the bottom of the mug to **snag** the last bit of **chocolate.**

Mom asked me where my manners were and I told her, "Invisible!" The Space Invader said he did the same thing when he was my age. Mom said he was joking, because he always had good manners as a kid. I'm not so sure about that. Right after we finished our hot chocolate, Mom told me to show Uncle Dug where he was sleeping because he had been up for almost twenty hours. I dashed to my room to rip down the sign I had taped on the bottom bunk that said:

YOU ARE **NOT** WELCOME, SPACE INVADER!

After Uncle Dug and I were both in our bunks and the lights were off, I heard Mom open my bedroom door. She quietly walked over to my bed, almost bumping into Uncle Dug's foot that was hanging off the lower bunk. She gave me a hug and whispered how happy she was that I'd had a change of heart about her brother.

I told her, "He's now my Uncle Dug and not the Space Invader."

And I really meant it.

Pancakes and Bacon

I woke up smelling pancakes and bacon this morning. Uncle Dug and Mom were in the kitchen sharing stories about life growing up in Texas. I heard Mom tell George not to bring any of his grasshoppers to the breakfast table. For the first time in a long time, it feels really nice to have a guy around.

Once I showed up, Uncle Dug gave me a high-five and said he was glad to see both George and me. He told us he had some surprise plans for the day. I wondered what those could be. George said he wanted to go grasshopper hunting or on a dinosaur dig. We didn't do either of those things, but we went on a hike and got in a little fishing. Even Mom!

None of us caught anything, but we did laugh a lot.

Maybe that's what scared the fish away. Uncle Dug told us some great jokes, just like Mom does when she's in the right mood—which is usually when a bowl of ice cream is in front of her.

Might Be a Prophet

I stayed late after school to work on my science project. What I want to do is to discover a way that humans can live successfully on Mars. I'm designing some special geodesic domes (for living in) and protective space suits (for wearing) since the average temperature on Mars is -81 degrees.

I've been laying the plan for the domes out in a program on the computer and it's coming together perfectly. My blueprint needs to be in place before I use the science department's 3D printer. Mr. Bullard thinks I have another shot at first place. It always feels good to win, but what really matters is that I do a great job on my project. When Mom hears me say this, she tells me I have a mature attitude.

But whenever I'm around **Mugersnot,** that attitude disappears.

YOU HAVE A MATURE ATTITUDE.

Mugersnot has been on my mind, even though I didn't see him around school today. I hear he's been working on his science project and wants to win big this year.

Mom let me know this morning that Uncle Dug wouldn't be around this afternoon. He's at the library doing research. I'll take Buckles and head to the creek to do some fishing before dinner.

I wonder what Aunt Gertie will burn— I mean, cook.

I might be a prophet. One of those guys who calls it before it happens. I came home from fishing and found out that Aunt Gertie had charcoaled dinner. The beef in the frying pan was burnt because she forgot about it after answering a call from her sister. It was the smoke pouring out of our kitchen windows that caught my attention. I dropped my trout on the grass and ran inside the house. It was a good thing that Uncle Dug was already working on the problem. He had come home early from the library and had set up fans to blow the smoke out. Aunt Gertie must have said she was sorry at least a dozen times. I told her not to worry and it wasn't that big of a deal because she didn't burn the house down.

When the air finally cleared, Uncle Dug asked...

...if he could help me clean and cut my catch.

Aunt Gertie asked if she could make trout stroganoff. George said he hates eating fish. Aunt Gertie told him just to put a lot of ketchup on it. During dinner, Uncle Dug told Aunt Gertie how tasty her trout stroganoff was, and, of course, that made her feel a whole lot better.

Mom will definitely hear about it when she wakes up tomorrow morning. Aunt Gertie will tell her how she was frying beef and forgot about it while talking on the phone with her sister, Polly.

Then she'll **hear** how Aunt Polly's super-old cat, Whiskers, met her end by **tumbling** off a roof.

Mom's aunts live down the street, but Aunt Gertie is the only one who visits every day and tries to help out. Aunt Polly doesn't because she's busy taking care of strays and volunteering at the animal shelter. Mom will be more upset about that burnt pan than Whiskers going on to his heavenly house. She doesn't like cats because she's allergic to them. Now she'll have a new worry. She will start thinking Aunt Gertie is getting too scatterbrained to take care of us. But I'll tell Mom not to worry about that because Aunt Gertie has always been that way. She's the pancake type, flipping here and flipping there, forgetting this and forgetting that.

Uncle Dug said everyone can be forgetful and get distracted and do dumb things. It's not worth getting upset about. Aunt Gertie gave him a hug and said that's why she likes him the best out of all her family. I'll have to admit, he was really chill about everything, especially when...

...he **scrubbed** the charcoal-burnt pan until it **looked** new again.

The Ancient Dude
and the Ancient Book

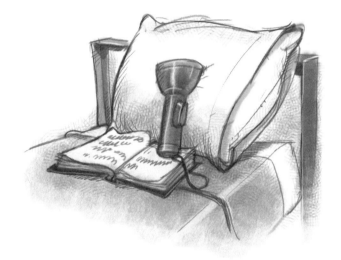

I'm wide awake and stoked about my bunk talk with Uncle Dug tonight. I have to write it down before I forget and my flashlight batteries wear out.

I never imagined I would tell someone in my family about my problems with Mugersnot. I told Uncle Dug what the bully had been up to and how he is my worst enemy. Now he knows all the awful things Mugersnot has done—stuff no one else knows, not Flynn, not Buckles, and not even this journal.

After I was done wearing his ears out, he told me how sorry he was for everything I've gone through. He made me feel better by telling me how bullies have been around for thousands of years. My battle isn't new. He reminded me that every generation has had their share of bullies.

I wonder if Mom had a **bully** on her back when she was **my age** and if Aunt Gertie had one too.

Uncle Dug said when he was *my* age, he struggled with bullies. That is, until he learned an incredible secret.

My ears **opened** wide, and so did my **mouth**.

I asked, "What's the secret?" Uncle Dug laughed and told me I'd have to wait and grow some patience because the incredible secret is woven into an unbelievable story about an awesome bully buster. Maybe the answer to my bully problems isn't trying to convince Flynn to make my bully busting video after all.

Uncle Dug was pretty pumped to tell me a true story about an ancient dude who knew the incredible secret of how to bust a bully. Before he got started, he told me the name of the ancient dude was Nehemiah, and he lived 2,500 years ago.

I wasn't sure if I wanted to know about someone who lived that long ago, but Uncle Dug's excitement told me I should at least hear him out. So I did. He started by saying that Nehemiah was a leader of a group of people called the Israelites. Nehemiah was a kind of ancient hero, who did important work but had a tough time doing it because bullies tried to stop him. But with the power of the incredible secret, Nehemiah was able to get the job done.

I was ready to hear more about this ancient dude and his story. I asked Uncle Dug where he had heard the story. He told me I could read about it in an ancient book called the Bible. Yikes! That's the same book Aunt Gertie's Sermonator uses at church. I let Uncle Dug know that I didn't have the ancient book, and I wasn't planning on picking it up anytime soon. I always thought it was only for people, like Aunt Gertie, who have nothing better to read, not for cool, smart people like me. I can't believe that Uncle Dug, the brainy archeologist, believes in the ancient dude and the ancient book. He says the stories are not fairy tales but have a lot of history behind them that's supported by archeological evidence.

I was blown away.

Right then, George came into my room and wanted to join our conversation. He climbed up to my bunk and plopped himself down. Uncle Dug told George he was happy to see him. I wasn't.

I told George that I was only okay with him hanging out with us as long as he didn't bring any of his grasshoppers along. He didn't say anything, so I guessed that meant he didn't have those green hoppers stuffed in his pajamas somewhere.

Uncle Dug started Nehemiah's story by giving us a little background. He told us that thousands of years ago in the Middle East, there were lots of farmers and animal herders who formed different tribes. Soon, some of the bigger tribes took over the weaker ones. I wonder if Mugersnot's "tribe" is going to take me over. I asked Uncle Dug how archaeologists figure out which tribe lived where and who was in charge. That's when he told me that they look at all kinds of stones, coins, scrolls, and pieces of pottery, and they also study the ancient book to find locations where they might do some digging.

Uncle Dug said the **ancient** book has given him all kinds of **places** and **locations** to find out about...

...groups like the Hittites, the Philistines, and the Israelites. He let us know that the Israelite tribe always kept going, no matter how often bigger tribes like the Philistines tried to crush them. It was like the Israelites had some strange, supernatural force behind them.

I didn't want to think about everything I was hearing as really true, but being a science facts kind of guy, I'm pretty curious to learn more.

Uncle Dug explained how the ancient book tells the story of the Heavenly King, who is the Creator of everyone and everything. The Heavenly King made Himself known to a man named Abraham who became a father of a small tribe that was later called the Israelites. This small tribe was turned into a great nation by the Heavenly King. He gave them wise rules to live by that

75

lined up with how they were made—to honor the Heavenly King and treat themselves and others with kindness and respect. If not, life for the Israelites would be full of struggle and heartache. If they followed the Heavenly King's wise ways, then the Israelites would live long and prosper. Uncle Dug also said the Heavenly King had lots of good things for the Israelites and...

...He gave them **wonderful** gifts, but they didn't always **appreciate** them or say thank you!

George brought up how he really liked last year's Christmas gifts and how he thanked Aunt Gertie and Mom, especially for the new net to catch his grasshoppers in.

One of the Heavenly King's gifts was the Promised Land. It was a land so lush and beautiful the Israelites said it was the "land of milk and honey." Later on, the amazing land was called Israel.

The Israelites worked hard to farm the land, graze cattle and sheep, and build up cities, including Jerusalem, which became Israel's capital. The Israelites made a temple there to worship the Heavenly King.

I was surprised when Uncle Dug told George and me that the Israelites bucked big time even though they had been given so much. Instead of being happy for everything they'd gotten and honoring the Heavenly King for His generosity, they hurt Him by making up their own rules about living life. Many times, they copied the ways of the other tribes and nations that lived around them instead of showing them the truth of the Heavenly King and His right ways of living.

Uncle Dug told us how heartbroken the Heavenly King was over Israel's choice to turn from Him. He continued to warn them about the serious consequences of doing life their way. If the Israelites didn't do a U-turn, they would be taken out by their enemies and lose their beautiful land. But the Israelites chose to ignore the Heavenly King's warning and roadmap for life, and instead, continued following the roadmaps of the nations around them.

Sometimes, like the Israelites, I want to make up my own rules. I thought about the choice I have to follow Mom's rules. The problem is that when I don't go along with them, annoying consequences come my way. I'm grounded and I can't go fishing and I'm not allowed to watch TV, play video games, or draw on my iPad. Then Mom sends me to my room to write sentences about how I should act. If I'm breaking a whole bunch of rules,

I can't have any **sweets,** which means **no** donuts or Pop-Tarts.

Mom's rules
① Make your Bed.
② Keep your room tidy.
③ Have a good Attitude.
④ Don't talk back.
⑤ Be nice to your brother.
⑥ Eat your vegetables.
⑦ Do your Homework.
⑧ Read a book for 30 minutes everyday.

Just when I was about to ask Uncle Dug a question, I saw it. A grasshopper jumping on my bed. I looked at George and told him, "You know my rule! NO GRASSHOPPERS IN MY BED! Get it and go!" He got the little guy and left, but not before he double pinky promised that he wouldn't bring any along next time. I don't know if I can believe him.

Wednesday May 3

Hard Time Believing

I'm annoyed that George brought a grasshopper into my room last night. I'm also annoyed about Mugersnot almost tripping me in the hallway after lunch. After he tried, I told him that he was a big fat loser, and, when I did, his goons circled me and started yelling,

"BEEP-BEEP-LOSER, BEEP-BEEP-LOSER!"

I ran into Mr. Bullard's class, feeling sick. I got to go home early.

I keep thinking about Uncle Dug's story last night. I'm trying to get my head wrapped around what he's been telling me, especially how the ancient book has facts about real people, places, and times. I'm still having a hard time believing that archeology backs up the ancient book. He's always assuring me that there's a lot of evidence in the historical record for the ancient book's reliability. That's why he takes the story about the Heavenly King seriously. I remember Uncle Dug saying that anyone who followed the ancient book's wise ways, whether they were a king or a farmer, had their life changed for good. I'm not so sure what those ways are,

but I sure hope one of them isn't having to eat runny eggs.

78

At our bunk talk time tonight (I'm gonna call it "BT"), Uncle Dug reminded George and me again about how the Israelites were set on their own ways instead of the Heavenly King's wise ways. I let George know that it isn't wise to bring his grasshoppers into my room, and, if he does, I might give him a time-out. Uncle Dug laughed and said that I shouldn't be so upset. I told him, "George isn't leaving any grasshoppers on your pillow."

Uncle Dug threw his pillow up at me, and I threw it back. He said, "TRUCE!" Then he quickly moved on by telling more of the ancient story.

The Israelites were going into a time-out. They had to pay the price for following their own rules, so a powerful king was going to come on the scene and take over their land. I thought about Mom grounding me when I talk back to her.

At least she has never sent a **king** to take over my **room.**

The Assyrians were a nasty bunch and they turned the Israelites homeland into a place where almost everyone had to work as a slave. George interrupted and said that was a "hard time-out!"

Uncle Dug agreed. I asked Uncle Dug if there was any artifact proving Israel was captured by the Assyrians. He said I asked a great question and the answer was a most definite "YES!" There's a large six foot, four-sided monument, made of black limestone that's in the British Museum. The monument is called an obelisk, and there's an engraving on it of Israel's king Jehu bowing low to the Assyrian king.

Uncle Dug wanted me to know that as hard as it was for Israel to be conquered by the Assyrians, they still didn't learn their lesson. George asked if they learned a lesson about not bringing any grasshoppers around the Heavenly King. Uncle Dug started to laugh, and I couldn't help but think that's what my five-year-old brother would say for sure!

The Israelites should have learned that following the wise ways of the Heavenly King would bring them peace and good things, and bucking up and going their own way would bring them disaster and suffering. But they didn't learn.

Uncle Dug said that because the Israelites continued to ignore the wise rules and do their own thing, another king showed up years later. This king was a Babylonian dude, King Nebuchadnezzar, or King Nebbie as I'll call him. Uncle Dug said that Israel's best and brightest people were captured by King Nebbie and carted away from their beautiful homeland to a distant land called Babylon, almost eight hundred miles away. Only the poor Israelites were left behind.

I had **reached** my fill for the night when George let one of his **grasshoppers** out of his hand. It **jumped** on my nose!

George grabbed it quickly, and jumped off my bunk. I was too tired to care.

I drifted off to **sleep** thinking about the things **Uncle Dug** was saying...

...and wondering if I would ever hear about the incredible secret of how to bust a bully.

I Still Can't Stop Thinking

I saw Flynn after school today and asked him if he knew anything about people who used the Bible for archaeology. He said that he had read a little about it, and then he changed the subject and started talking about his chess game.

I still can't stop thinking about what Uncle Dug was telling George and me last night. I don't know if I can really believe what he's saying, especially about an ancient dude who has the incredible secret of bully busting. Mugersnot isn't getting any easier to be around. In Mr. Bullard's class, he was telling Prudence Glummer that I like her. He even told the class that our family is so poor that we can't buy electricity and we have to use candles.

Once we got settled into our bunks after dinner and the dishes were done, I reminded Uncle Dug that he hadn't finished his story about what happened to the Israelites after their time-outs. He laughed and said I must be really interested in the ancient dude and the ancient book. I told him the only reason I'm staying interested is because I want to find out how to bust a bully with the incredible secret. Uncle Dug said, "Keep being patient. You'll find out soon enough!" Then he told me how the ancient book has other heroes in it besides Nehemiah who also used the power of the incredible secret to conquer their own bullies.

He told me about a **dude** named David who killed a **giant**...

...with a rock, and how a blind guy named Samson brought the roof down on the heads of his enemies.

Hearing just a little about those heroes made me even more curious about Nehemiah and his battle with bullies. I wanted to get back to where Uncle Dug had left off last night. He asked what I remembered so far. I told him the Israelites rebelled against the Heavenly King's wise ways, and so the Assyrians conquered them and they got put into a time-out. There was an archaeological record for that happening. A carved little drawing was made on a black column and it showed an Israelite king dude named Jehu bowing down before some Assyrian king dude. Uncle Dug liked how I put it and said I had a good memory. Then he asked me what king conquered the Israelites the second time. I wasn't sure about that one. Uncle Dug gave me a clue and said the king's name was close to the word 'nebulous' (which means hazy). Then my brain kicked in and I said, "King Nebbie!" the Babylonian dude. Uncle Dug threw a pillow up in the air and bellowed, "You're right, Andy!"

That's when George walked into my room and caught the pillow. He gave it back to Uncle Dug and then he held up his hands to let me know he didn't have any green hoppers. I asked him if he was double pinky promising me and he said he was, so I let him climb up to my bunk.

Uncle Dug **started** the **ancient** story back up...

...and reminded George and me that the Babylonian King Nebbie left the poor Israelites behind in Jerusalem. George piped in and said that was because they didn't have any money. Uncle Dug said that was partly true. King Nebbie needed the poor to care for the land. If it was totally abandoned it would soon be covered in weeds and filled with wild animals. The important thing to know was that King Nebbie only took the Israelites who were rich, smart, and leaders. After rounding them up, he marched them eight hundred miles to Babylon. Uncle Dug called that being "exiled." George asked him what 'exited' meant. Uncle Dug laughed and said the word was "EXILED," and that it meant being forced to leave your homeland and live in a place far away.

I think being exiled would be pretty awful but maybe it wouldn't be too bad as long as I was away from Mugersnot.

Uncle Dug went on and told us King Nebbie wanted to humiliate the Israelites, so he tore down their temple in Jerusalem and turned their city wall and gates into rubble and ashes. "Would the wall ever be rebuilt?" I asked Uncle Dug. He said I'd have to wait for more of the story. He said not to worry because everything he's told us so far is important background for Nehemiah's story. I sure hope we get to hear it all soon before my hair turns white. I really want to know about how this ancient dude wielded the power of the incredible secret to battle his bullies.

Uncle Dug talked about how big of a deal walls were in the time of Nehemiah. All the largest cities had walls around them to make it harder for their enemies to attack. A city without a wall had no protection. Some of the walls were so wide that people built houses on them.

Uncle Dug must have read my thoughts because that's when he told George and me that archaeologists had found a bunch of cuneiform tablets, which are like clay blocks with letters stamped into them,

I asked Uncle Dug if the poor people who were left behind got all the rich people's money. He said, "NO!" All of it went into the "Bank of Babylon." I still couldn't get over how much the Israelites lost because of their rebellion against the Heavenly King's wise ways.

I wondered how the Israelites might have felt living in a strange land so far from their home. Uncle Dug said it was written in the ancient book that, "By the rivers of Babylon we sat and cried when we remembered Jerusalem." The Israelites were crying rivers of tears because their city Jerusalem, its temple, and its wall were in ruins. Life would never be the same for them again. The Israelites would be in Babylon for a long time-out.

I asked Uncle Dug how he knew all this was true. He answered, "Archaeology!" He told George and me how archaeologists had dug up the ancient city of Babylon. They discovered cool sculptures and walls full of inscriptions that talked about King Nebbie and his takeover of most of the ancient world. Archaeologists also found clay tablets written in cuneiform, which Uncle Dug said is wedge-shaped writing made with sticks on soft clay. These clay tablets are known as the "Babylonian Chronicles." They're a bunch of very old tablets that recorded the big events in Babylonian history. They also show where the exiled Israelites had resettled in Babylon. I wondered if the Babylonian Chronicles matched up with the ancient book. Uncle Dug read my thoughts because he said,

"The Chronicles **absolutely** match up with the ancient book's **story** of the Israelites exile to Babylon.

I looked over at George and he was already asleep. Uncle Dug took him back to his hammock. I was happy that he didn't leave any of his hoppers behind. George honored his double pinky promise. Maybe he really is changing his ways.

Exiled

I woke up from a nightmare. I was exiled from Woodside Junior High. Mugersnot was the principal and he banished me to a junior high school in Alaska where his mean twin brother, Brutus, was the assistant principal. Brutus threw frozen bananas at me, turned me into a snowman, and put a carrot on my face for a nose.

Uncle Dug asked if I was okay this morning after he heard me mumbling in my sleep, "It's cold, Brutus, stop it!" I didn't tell Uncle Dug about my nightmare, but I did ask him if he would let me know what Nehemiah did to beat his bullies. That's when he laughed and told me I was "persistent." He said he wasn't going to give me the incredible secret until it was the right time. I still had to know a bunch of stuff about Nehemiah first. I guess that makes sense, it's just not what I wanted to hear. Uncle Dug grinned and told me that in the end, I would be happy he didn't tell me right away. I wasn't so sure about that, but I was sure that I was going to be late for school if I didn't get up and out the door soon.

I was pretty stoked that Mugersnot wasn't around school today. I breezed through the day without having to deal with any of his nasty looks in science class. The best part of my day was getting home and hanging out with Uncle Dug. When I walked into the kitchen, I saw him fixing our leaky faucet. He turned around and said, "No more leaking!" I said, "That's cool, but...

...how about **leaking** some more about **Nehemiah?"**

Uncle Dug poured us a couple of glasses of lemonade and we sat down at the table. I told him, "I'm all ears!" and just about knocked over my glass in excitement, but Uncle Dug stopped it from crashing to the floor. He told me that he would get to his story during our BT time since he had to head out to do some more research at the library.

When Uncle Dug got home from the library and after we finished dinner, George and I settled on my bunk for BT time. Uncle Dug brought up another king named Cyrus. He was an important Persian dude because, without him on the scene, Nehemiah would not have been able to do his great work. That work depended on Israel rebuilding the destroyed temple and on the Israelites returning to the Heavenly King with the help of a dude named Ezra.

Uncle Dug said it was the Persian king Cyrus who made all this possible. He did that by conquering the Babylonians and taking over Jerusalem after King Nebbie had it for a long time.

Some people believe that the only reason King Cyrus agreed to let the Israelites rebuild their temple was because he was scared of being killed by another king who might invade the land and take him out. King Cyrus thought that if he paid for the rebuilding of the Israelite's temple, he would gain favor from their Heavenly King and he would have extra protection from anything bad happening to him. So Cyrus sent an Israelite named Zerubbabel back to Jerusalem with 42,000 other Israelites to start rebuilding the temple.

When the people living in the land around Jerusalem saw Zerubbabel and the returning Israelites laying the foundation for the temple, they started complaining to each other and to the Persian rulers. They said mean things to discourage the Israelites so the work would stop. I couldn't help but think that what the Israelites were going through was like what I'm going through with Mugersnot and his goons.

Uncle Dug said the foreign tribes bribed the Persian rulers to make life miserable for the Israelites, and after eighteen years of putting up with it, the Israelites were about ready to give up. George said the Israelites were scaredy cats. But Uncle Dug said the biggest scaredy cat was their leader Zerubbabel, who let the bullies' mean words get to him. He didn't look to the Heavenly King for wisdom, strength, and courage.

The Israelites' weak faith was strengthened when two dudes, Haggai and Zechariah, arrived. They encouraged the Israelites to trust in the Heavenly King and not be afraid to finish the work. Uncle Dug said, from then on, ...

...the Israelites worked fast with a lot of heart, and completed the temple in just two years.

The Israelites were so excited about their new temple that they had a celebration party. The younger generation of Israelites were seeing the Heavenly King's temple for the first time! The old people who remembered the original temple cried because the rebuilt temple was not as beautiful. They were disappointed but still glad they had a temple to worship in!

Uncle Dug said the foundation of Zerubbabel's temple is still in Jerusalem and that he has seen it. George said he wanted to see it too!

I'm not so sure about checking out a bunch of rubble, rocks, and dirt.

An Earful

I spent the day fishing with Buckles and Flynn. I caught three fish and Flynn caught one. He probably wouldn't have caught any if I hadn't helped him reel it in. He doesn't like fishing as much as I do, and he said he was doing me a favor by going with me to the creek.

During dinner, Aunt Gertie told us that Uncle Dug was coming in later tonight after doing some research at the Metropolitan Museum in New York City. I couldn't wait to get an earful after he was home. I was hoping he was down for BT time.

When George and I finished washing the dishes, Uncle Dug walked in the door. He was excited to tell us about his day, but not before he asked us about ours. George said he found a long-horned grasshopper. I sure hope he doesn't bring that guy into my room. I told Uncle Dug it was a decent day because I got to go fishing with Flynn and Buckles.

It didn't take long to settle into our bunks and as soon as we did, Uncle Dug told us about how he got permission from the top officials at the museum to study something called the Cyrus Cylinder. I wasn't sure why he would be so stoked about a clay cylinder that was only nine inches long and four inches wide. George asked if it was like playdough. Uncle Dug said it was more like mud that's baked to make it hard. The cylinder was covered in cuneiform writing, those wedge-shaped characters. George asked if it had any drawings of grasshoppers on it. Uncle Dug laughed and said, "No!"

What Uncle Dug told us about the **Cyrus Cylinder** was pretty interesting...

...and seemed to back up what the ancient book was saying about the Israelites. He said the writing on the cylinder talked about how the Persian king Cyrus conquered Babylon. The cylinder also had writing on it about King Cyrus bragging on himself for being a perfect ruler.

I asked Uncle Dug when Nehemiah would finally come on the scene. He said not for almost another hundred years! In that case, I realized Cyrus must have lived to be more than one hundred years old. I told Uncle Dug I hoped it wouldn't be one hundred years before I could hear about the ancient dude and the incredible secret.

Uncle Dug **laughed** and **continued** the story.

A long line of kings came after Cyrus, then a king named Artaxerxes arrived. I'll call him Artie. It was King Artie who sent Ezra to teach the Israelites about the Heavenly King's wise ways. Ezra arrived almost sixty years after Zerubbabel finished the temple and then, thirteen years after Ezra, Nehemiah arrived.

— . — . — . — · — · — . — . —

"Finally, it's about time!" I said, tossing a pillow in the air. George caught it. He looked excited too that Nehemiah was now in the story. I asked why it took so long. Uncle Dug said the Heavenly King's ways and timing are not always what we think they should be, but He always knows best.

Then I told Uncle Dug how Mugersnot was continuing to annoy me. When I pass him in the hallway at school, he often shoots small, hard peas at me with a plastic spoon.

George asked Uncle Dug if Nehemiah had peas shot at him by his bullies.

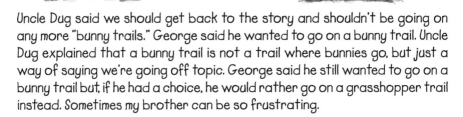

Uncle Dug said we should get back to the story and shouldn't be going on any more "bunny trails." George said he wanted to go on a bunny trail. Uncle Dug explained that a bunny trail is not a trail where bunnies go, but just a way of saying we're going off topic. George said he still wanted to go on a bunny trail but, if he had a choice, he would rather go on a grasshopper trail instead. Sometimes my brother can be so frustrating.

Uncle Dug said that in those thirteen years before Nehemiah arrived, Ezra picked judges to help the Israelites treat each other with fairness. George thought that was a pretty good idea and Uncle Dug should be a judge and decide whether it's fair for me to not let his grasshoppers come into my room. Uncle Dug laughed and said he wasn't ready to be a judge about that.

During those years when Ezra was busy teaching the Israelites about the Heavenly King's wise ways, Nehemiah was serving as a cupbearer to the Persian king Artie, back in Babylon.

Uncle Dug said that archeologists found a **fragment** of the Nehemiah story...

...on a scroll from the Qumran Caves in Egypt. I didn't know what to think about that. George said he wanted a copy of the scroll.

I asked Uncle Dug what a cupbearer does. He said they taste the king's food and drink before it's served to the king just in case one of the king's enemies tried to poison him.

George said that he'd like a **cupbearer** too...

...not just to taste Aunt Gertie's vegetables for him, but to eat them all for him too. I said that would be better than George throwing them away in the trash can.

Uncle Dug gave George a funny look before he explained how Nehemiah was like a teacher's pet, someone King Artie of Babylon could trust and count on. They were good friends and they talked about lots of things, including their families' histories. Nehemiah was not like the other rebellious Israelites. He had a heart for the Heavenly King and wanted to live by His wise ways.

One day, Nehemiah's brother and some other Israelites came to visit Nehemiah from Jerusalem, which was eight hundred miles away. They shared good news and bad news. The good news was that Jerusalem's temple had been rebuilt. The bad news was that Jerusalem's wall was still down and its gates had been burned. George asked why this was bad news. Uncle Dug had already told us about the importance of city walls but George forgot, so Uncle Dug reminded him that the enemies of Jerusalem could easily attack them since they had no protective wall around their city.

Hearing such terrible news from his brother and friends made Nehemiah cry. I was surprised anyone would cry over a broken-down wall.

"Real men do cry," Uncle Dug said.

I didn't know what to say to that, but I was even more shocked when Uncle Dug said that Nehemiah didn't eat for days. I couldn't imagine how someone who had so much food around him wouldn't eat anything, not even a Pop-Tart! Uncle Dug said Nehemiah was fasting from food so he could focus on talking to the Heavenly King about what was bothering him.

After fasting, Nehemiah decided he wanted to change his address and move eight hundred miles to Jerusalem. George asked if that's what he did. Uncle Dug said, "Not right away."

First, Nehemiah waited and **humbled** himself before the Heavenly King.

I asked if Nehemiah was going to restore the wall. Uncle Dug pulled out a sketch of the ancient city of Jerusalem, then turned on a flashlight and shined it on the drawing. It showed what the wall around the city of Jerusalem looked like before it was destroyed and how there were ten separate entrance gates. Uncle Dug said the wall was about two and a half miles long, eight feet thick, and thirty-nine feet tall. The oak tree in my front yard is about that high. George stared at the sketch and said it would take a giant grasshopper to jump over that wall.

I asked Uncle Dug again if **Nehemiah** was going to **restore** the wall.

I waited for an answer. For a second I thought he was thinking deeply, but he wasn't. He was sleeping deeply, calling the hogs. Then I looked over at George and heard him calling those hogs too, but not as loud. There I was, hearing a chorus of hog-callers. I'd had enough and woke George up and helped him to his hammock. He was full of groggy and grumble, but he wasn't so out of it that he didn't make sure to leave two grasshoppers on my pillow.

I really don't know what I'm **going** to do about George and his **hoppers.**

Honest Talk

Uncle Dug asked if we would ride with him and Aunt Gertie to church. George and I both looked at each other and then back at Uncle Dug. We told him,

"NO!"

After Uncle Dug got home from church, he took George and me out to hit some baseballs. I hit way more than George, but he wasn't that into it because all he wanted to do was collect grasshoppers.

When we settled down for our BT time, Uncle Dug reminded us how sad Nehemiah was over Jerusalem's broken-down wall and burned gates and how, even though it made him cry, he was no wimp. I didn't want to sound impatient, but I asked again whether Nehemiah was going to rebuild Jerusalem's wall and gates. Uncle Dug started to laugh and said, "Yes, Andy, but not without some real help. Nehemiah knew he was going to be in for a battle with bullies and he would need the power of the incredible secret." I was all ears, now!

Before Nehemiah could leave Babylon and travel to Jerusalem, he needed King Artie's permission. George said that Nehemiah would need good shoes because Jerusalem was eight hundred miles away. I told him Nehemiah probably rode a horse. Uncle Dug said I was right but there was a hitch in

Nehemiah's plan. There was no guarantee King Artie would let Nehemiah go—especially when he would be gone a long time from his duties as cupbearer.

Nehemiah had to have an **honest** talk with the Heavenly King.

Uncle Dug told George and me that Nehemiah's 'honest talk' is called prayer. I didn't know much about that because I'm not really the praying kind of person, and I thought prayer only happened in church. Uncle Dug said prayer can happen anytime and anyplace because the Heavenly King is always around and ready to hear from us. All it takes is bringing a humble you to the one and only Heavenly King, and speaking honestly about what's on your mind and heart.

Uncle Dug told me that when you're talking to the Heavenly King, you should always ask for wisdom to know the right thing to do. When you're done praying, you should be at rest because you can trust the Heavenly King to do what's best, even if it is different than what you expect. Thank Him for His answer in advance and tell Him how great and awesome He is. After all, He deserves it. He is the true Creator of the universe.

THANKS

Just when I was thinking it would be interesting to hear the real honest prayer of Nehemiah, Uncle Dug brought out a small black book and said, "This is the 'ancient book,' but most people know it as the Bible." He told us that it has the words of life and guides him with the wisdom and truth that comes from the Creator, the Heavenly King. It was written by over forty different authors in three languages over 1500 years. The Heavenly King helped each of the writers to write the history of His people and their relationship to Him.

I thumbed through it. I had no idea they made Bibles pocket-sized. I gave it back to Uncle Dug, and then he quickly turned to a page and said, "Here it is! Nehemiah's prayer." I can't remember it exactly, but this is what stands out in my mind...

Heavenly King,
Hear this prayer
You are So AWESOME!
You Rescued us when we
were in a tight place.
You never flake out
on your promises
to ANYONE who loves
and follows you with
all their HEART.
ALL of us ISRAELITES,
even my own family,
have messed UP and
went OUR OWN WAY AND
got INTO TROUBLE. YOU
ToLD us that if we
obeyed You that you
WOULD BLESS US.
Please HELP THE KiNG,
Be kind to me and let
me go to Jerusalem to
Rebuild the wall and
the gates.

I asked Uncle Dug if Nehemiah's prayer was answered.

"Stay tuned," Uncle Dug said, "because there's a **whole** lot more to the story. We're just getting started."

I turned to George and asked him to hold up his hands to make sure he didn't have any grasshoppers in them before he left my bunk. He had a little one in his left hand and I made sure he took it with him.

Day Off

School is closed today. The teachers have a meeting. I'd love to go to one of those, just to snag a donut or two.

Since I have the day off, that means no Mugersnot battles! Instead, I'll be working on my science project. The best part of the day already happened. I had breakfast with Uncle Dug. Mom left early to clean a house, so it was just Uncle Dug, George, and me hanging out eating the next best thing to donuts—Pop-Tarts! Uncle Dug fried some eggs too. I asked him to make the yolks extra hard so we wouldn't need straws to eat them. He had no problem doing that. They came out like rubber balls.

I could have **bounced** them around the kitchen.

Once we finished breakfast, I asked Uncle Dug if the Heavenly King answered Nehemiah's honest prayer. He said he didn't want to spoil the story and I would find out for myself soon enough. That sounded fair and we high-fived on it! But Uncle Dug did give me a hint and said that Nehemiah got a paid working vacation to go to Jerusalem to rebuild the walls and gates. The Persian King Artie not only covered all of Nehemiah's expenses, but he also gave him heavy-duty protection while he traveled, with army officers and horsemen surrounding him. I couldn't help but think how great it would be if I had mounted bodyguards shielding me from Mugersnot.

Uncle Dug also said that Nehemiah carried royal letters telling the local governors to protect him as he passed through their territories.

"Protect me!"

He also had a letter from King Artie to the manager of the royal forest. The letter said to give Nehemiah wood for the gates and for the city wall. If that wasn't awesome enough, Nehemiah asked King Artie for extra wood to build a house for himself. King Artie agreed. I have to admit Nehemiah's honest prayer was definitely answered and he got more good than he asked for.

I wonder if the Heavenly King sent down cartloads of donuts and Pop-Tarts.

Now, that would be **cool!**

Tuesday may 9

Space Huts

I was proud of myself for showing what Aunt Gertie calls "self-restraint." She tells me to use it to keep myself from doing something I shouldn't do, like hurting another person. I was in the school hallway standing behind a cement post when Mugersnot walked past me mumbling to himself. I was out of his view, so he was an easy target. I could have easily pummeled him with pink erasers. But I didn't. Instead, I let him pass quietly.

I don't know **why**, but I felt **bad** for him.

I'm seriously thinking about what Uncle Dug has been telling George and me during our BT time. I can't help but keep wondering about the incredible secret.

If I can use it to stop Mugersnot's attacks, I want to know what it is, and how I can put it into action ASAP. I want to ask Uncle Dug some more about it, but I don't want to bug him too much. I just have to believe that he'll tell me at the right time. So far, I've learned this about Uncle Dug: He's a "what you see is what you get" kind of a guy, and he's really nice and helpful. A couple of days ago, I watched Uncle Dug do some dirty work.

He **scooped** up Buckles' **brownies** and put them in the trash can.

I stayed late after school and went to Mr. Bullard's class to work on my science project. The science fair is less than two weeks away. My Mars project is not finished and it won't get done with me lying around in George's hammock drinking lemonade. I have to come up with a way to make cool space huts. I'm still researching to find out the best material for the huts and the wall to keep invaders out.

‒ ‒ ‒ ‒ ‒ ‒ ‒ ‒ ‒ ‒

On Earth, people build with cement, which is a mixture of lime, sand, and gravel. On Mars, it's different and you can't do that. Instead, scientists are planning to make concrete by mixing Mars' sulfur with other Martian soil. I've been designing a row of space huts, each looking like a geodesic dome. There could be a long tube connecting all of the huts. I want to ask Mr. Bullard if I can use his 3D printer to make the bricks for the wall around my Mars colony, the connecting tubes, and the domes. George has been asking me about 3D printing because he wants to print grasshoppers for my colony.

I told him that living grasshoppers can't be printed and, besides that, they can't live on Mars.

Before dinner tonight, Uncle Dug shot some hoops with us. Once we finished eating and washed the dishes, it was BT time. George came to my room, and I checked all his pockets and made him promise that he didn't have any grasshoppers. He crossed his heart and said he didn't. So George and I got comfortable and laid back on my bunk and pillows. I asked Uncle Dug what happened once Nehemiah made it to Jerusalem. Did the Israelites throw him a "Welcome to Jerusalem" party?

Uncle Dug laughed and said, "Nobody celebrated Nehemiah's arrival, especially a particular tricky trio." Their names were Sanballat, Tobiah, and Geshem. When they got wind that Nehemiah was in town, those dudes brewed trouble and got hopping mad about Nehemiah coming to rebuild Jerusalem's wall and city gates.

Sanballat was a Samaritan official, and Tobiah was an Ammonite official. Geshem was an Arabian who was the chief of his people, and maybe even a king of a local tribe.

Uncle Dug let us know that archeologists have **proof** that both Sanballat and Geshem were **real** people...

...because they were talked about in a papyrus that was found on a dig in Egypt. Uncle Dug told us he saw the papyrus at the Brooklyn Museum and is driving there tomorrow afternoon to go to a fancy dinner where he's going to give some kind of lecture. I'm sure going to miss him and our BT time.

104

Uncle Dug continued telling George and me more about Nehemiah. After he arrived in Jerusalem, Nehemiah stayed under the radar by slipping out late at night and riding on a donkey. He took a few Israelites with him to do some serious inspecting of the broken wall and burned gates without anyone knowing their true mission. Nehemiah rode the two and a half miles along the wall and went past all the gates. Everything was in terrible shape. Some gates were so broken down that...

...Nehemiah **struggled** to make it through them.

George asked what Nehemiah did after he finished riding around. Uncle Dug said Nehemiah talked to the Heavenly King about the mess Jerusalem was in and then went to bed and got some sleep. That's when the light in our room suddenly turned out.

George and I hollered so much that Uncle Dug turned it back on. He laughed and said, "Okay, we've only got a few more minutes before you boys need to sleep."

Uncle Dug told us that Nehemiah called a meeting the next day with the Israelite city officials, leaders, priests, nobles, and families. In this meeting, Nehemiah finally told them why he had come to Jerusalem. He talked about the favor he had received from King Artie. George said he knew what the favors were because the Heavenly King moved in King Artie's heart to make him extra nice. Nehemiah got permission to go to Jerusalem and he was given a big horse to ride so he wouldn't wear out his shoes, and King Artie gave him lots of good stuff, even if he didn't give him any grasshoppers.

Uncle Dug laughed and said the Israelites were super encouraged that the favor of the Heavenly King had been with Nehemiah. That was when they became excited about rebuilding the wall and gates. Nehemiah told the Israelites they would need to work together to get the job done, so he split the Israelites up into groups to divide the work. That made me think about how Aunt Gertie always says,

"Many hands make **light** work."

Once work on the wall and gates had started, the tricky trio mocked and ridiculed Nehemiah and the workers. "HA HA! What is this you are doing? Are you rebelling against the rulers and authorities?" Nehemiah stood his ground and answered,

"The Heavenly King stands with us. We are His servants and we'll start rebuilding. It's not your turf, but ours. So stay out!"

I asked Uncle Dug if he would agree with me that Nehemiah was one bold and fearless dude.

I waited for him to answer.

Then, I heard the chorus of hog-callers.

I took George back to his hammock and came back to bed. When I pulled my covers back, three beady-eyed grasshoppers stared straight up at me. I was grossed out after a squirt of brown gunk landed on top of my pillow. I hurriedly picked up all three of the annoying hoppers. I was miffed not only at George but at these characters too. They were as sassy and defiant as Sanballat, Tobiah, and Geshem. I tossed the nasty trio out my window and gave them a new home in our backyard.

I'm taking this up with George tomorrow!

Flatworms and Radiation

I stayed two hours after school today working in the science lab in Mr. Bullard's classroom. I wasn't alone. Mugersnot was around, hanging out in the computer lab. I overheard him asking about using the 3D printer. He didn't stay long, but found time to snap at me on his way out,

I wonder what Mugersnot is doing for his science project. He had a decent one last year. When I first saw it, I thought someone had made it for him or that he had bought it online. It looked really professional. He had a 3D presentation board, fantastic graphics, a ten-page report with statistics and analysis, colorful charts, and cool photos. His project was about the effects of radiation on household plants.

Mugersnot received a participation ribbon. He expected a blue ribbon, and when he didn't get it, he flipped out and jumped up and down like one of George's grasshoppers. I later found out that the reason Mugersnot didn't get the blue ribbon was because the judges believed he cheated. Flynn told me he felt embarrassed for Mugersnot when he watched his presentation, especially the part when the judges started asking questions.

Mugersnot hesitated and **stammered** like he didn't know what he was talking about.

My science project last year was about whether or not radiation from electronic household objects affects the ability of flatworms to regenerate. Flatworms are the only creature I know of that can regrow a body part after it has been chopped off. I tried proving how radiation from cell phones, TVs, computers, or Wi-Fi has some kind of effect, either positive or negative, on flatworms regrowing a part of their body. I didn't prove anything. My project was a DUD!

The really **crazy** thing is that the **judges** liked what I had done.

I couldn't believe it.

When Mugersnot found out I was the big winner, he was furious. He told me and everybody else that his science project was better than mine (and it probably was).

Mr. Bullard told me the difference between Mugersnot's project and mine was the way I talked to the judges about it. I seemed confident (even though I was sweating in my sneakers).

I was honest about what I knew and didn't know.

I told the judges I understood what I had set out to do and I figured out why it went wrong. I also answered their questions about what I could have done to make my project better, and I talked about whether or not I met my goals and what I saw as the future of my project. I was happy to tell the judges I had fun learning about flatworms. George probably had the most fun, because...

...he liked cutting them in half and watching them regrow the missing body part.

The judges could tell I was excited about my project and that I had put my heart and best effort into my work and presentation. Once again, Aunt Gertie's words proved right:

Mom just told me that Uncle Dug is going to be staying another week. She said it's because he likes hanging around us. That may be true, but I think it has more to do with him finishing his special research project. Whatever the reason, I couldn't be happier and neither George!

We talked about throwing a going-away party for him!

111

Not long ago, Uncle Dug told George and me that his first stop after he leaves us is Israel. Once he's there, he's planning to continue his research project. He'll be examining more of the Dead Sea Scroll fragments containing parts of the book of Nehemiah. The project sounds pretty cool. I told him I'll be packing myself in his suitcase if he leaves without telling me about Nehemiah's incredible secret and the Bully Buster. I don't know how much longer I can stand Mugersnot's heat. He's now leaving notes around Mr. Bullard's class saying nasty things about me. Uncle Dug promised that I would find out the incredible secret before he leaves. The weird thing is that I will really miss him when he goes.

I never thought in a zillion years I would ever be thinking that.

There's one more thing. I talked to George this afternoon about dropping off three annoying grasshoppers in my bed last night after he crossed his heart that he didn't have any. He told me he couldn't help himself. I said, "Then don't lie!" George hung his head down and told me he was only having a little fun.

Sometimes, I think **seriously** about **trading** in my little brother for a sister.

The Challenge

I'm still figuring out how to make a Mars colony work. I've laid out the physical design on a special software program. There are tons of problems to solve in order to make a successful life-sustaining colony on Mars.

That is the challenge! How do you come up with a pure air supply? Where do the water, food, heating, and cooling come from? How is waste managed and living space created? How are people going to get around? What about communication? Will there be cell phones? How are colonists going to be protected from sickness, disease, wind, and dust storms? In my design, I've included a wall around my colony to keep intruders out. There's one final important question I need to answer. How can living on Mars be fun?

I guess I could always build an ice skating rink on Mars' polar caps.

Tonight, during our BT time, Uncle Dug asked me questions about my science project. I told him I was planning to use a 3D printer. I asked him if he had ever used one in his work. He said he has, and it's a valuable tool that a lot of archaeologists are beginning to use. He brought up a story of how a Harvard team used a 3D printer to create a replica of a three-thousand-year-old smashed ceramic lion from lots of different photographs. That's wild! Uncle Dug was glad Mr. Bullard is letting me use the school's 3D printer to make my space huts, connecting tubes, and bricks for my wall.

Uncle Dug asked George and me if we were ready to start hearing more about Nehemiah's story. I threw a pillow at him, then he threw two at me and then George got into the action, and then there we were, all three of us having a full-blown pillow fight. Once our pillows were flattened, I bragged that I was the winner even though I really wasn't. Uncle Dug came in first. He had the most pillow whacks, and George came in second.

Once we got back into our bunks, Uncle Dug started talking again about Nehemiah's bullies, Sanballat, Tobiah, and Geshem. They were still angry about all the progress the Israelites were making on rebuilding the wall and gates. Sanballat got so worked up that he started insulting and mocking the Israelites in front of a crowd of his friends and army officers: "Yeah right, so what does this bunch of poor, feeble guys think they're doing? Do they really think they can build the wall in a single day by just offering a few prayers?...

I wondered if Nehemiah wanted to punch Sanballat in the face. If I were there, I would have tried, but maybe I wouldn't have because I haven't landed a punch or a kick in my battles with Mugersnot or even a good pillow whack on George or Uncle Dug. If Sanballat's teasing wasn't enough, Tobiah also started joking that...

...the stone wall that Nehemiah and the Israelites were building would collapse if even a fox walked along the top of it!

That's when I asked the most important question: "What did Nehemiah do to get back at the bullies? What was his battle plan?" Uncle Dug seemed to know what I was thinking, so he told me that Nehemiah used the power of the incredible secret.

Then from out of Uncle Dug's pocket came his little Bible. He flipped it open to the story of Nehemiah and started to read the prayer. I can't write it down exactly, but this is my best shot at remembering it.

Heavenly King, we are being teased and made fun of. Make their insults come back on the bullies' heads. Cart them off to another country. Don't ignore what they've been doing to your people, the ones who have been working so hard on the wall and gates.

I wondered if Nehemiah's prayer was answered. Uncle Dug said the Heavenly King wasn't done dealing with the bullies yet. The important thing for Nehemiah was keeping the workers inspired and encouraged. He kept a positive attitude, and soon the wall was built up to half of its height, about nineteen feet, in spite of the bullies.

I was expecting to hear a lot more about that, but Uncle Dug said nothing. He had fallen asleep, and George too. I guess the pillow fighting took it out of them.

I looked over at George. His eyes were closed and he had one of his grasshoppers in his hand. I was happy the annoying thing wasn't jumping on my pillow or squirting brown gunk in my face.

I knew what was **coming** next: the **hog-calling** chorus.

It came, and I was too tired to help George back to his bed. But I did toss that hopper out my window.

Aunt Gertie says, "If you can't beat 'em, join 'em," so I did. I crashed on the bunk with George and Uncle Dug. But that only works on some things. I'm not joining Mugersnot's gang of goons just because I can't beat them. Mom told me this morning that around midnight, when she came home from work, she heard noises coming from my bedroom. She wanted to see what was going on, so she went to my room and saw all three of us laid out fast asleep with our mouths wide open, whooping it up, calling the hogs. George was the whistler, Uncle Dug was the rumbler, and I was the wheezer.

Friday may 12

Cartwheeled All the Way Down

This morning at school Flynn told me something. He asked if I'd heard what happened to Mugersnot. My ears were burning with curiosity. Flynn goofed around, saying he would tell me only if I told him my chess strategy. He wanted to know how I put his king in check in two moves. I laughed. Since he's not giving me a video, he's not getting my two-move chess strategy.

Flynn ended up telling me what happened. He had been taking a makeup test in Mr. Bullard's room when he noticed Mugersnot working in the chemistry lab. When Mugersnot left, he had a large box in his arms that he had a hard time seeing around. Flynn wondered how Mugersnot was going to make it down the steep stairs. He didn't have to wonder long. On the very first step, Mugersnot lost his balance and cartwheeled all the way down. His box went flying high in the air and both Mugersnot and the box landed with a crashing thud at the bottom.

Flynn **yelled** for Mr. Bullard after seeing Mugersnot **sprawled** flat on his back,...

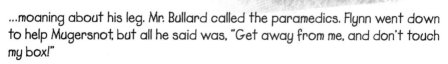

...moaning about his leg. Mr. Bullard called the paramedics. Flynn went down to help Mugersnot, but all he said was, "Get away from me, and don't touch my box!"

I wonder whether Mugersnot will be up to his old bully ways now that he'll likely be hobbling around with a cast. I'm super curious about what was so important to him in that box.

Today after school, Mr. Bullard took a careful look at my Mars colony design. He liked what I came up with, especially my wall and space huts shaped like geodesic domes.

I asked Mr. Bullard if I could use his 3D printer and he said, "Yes!" I also got to talk with him about using real sulfhur mixed with soil to make the bricks for my space huts, connecting tubes, and wall. To that, Mr. Bullard said no because it would be toxic and dangerous and would gum up the printer. Instead, I should use the plastic pellets in the 3D printer as my material, and then let the judges know why I think sulfur and Martian sand would be the best construction material for building on Mars.

If my 3D printing goes well, I'll be ready for the science fair. After struggling to solve those living-life-on-Mars problems, now the only thing left for me to do is to practice my speech for the judges. Maybe I'll get Flynn to hear my presentation.

At dinner, I took great delight in telling Uncle Dug the story of Mugersnot's accident. The worst bully in the universe got exactly what was coming to him. I expected Uncle Dug to give me a high five, but he didn't. Instead, he gave me a funny look and said, "Andy, never gloat over another person's downfall." Then Uncle Dug said something weird and awkward. He told me he would pray for Mugersnot to heal quickly, and that I should pray for him too! He said sometimes the bravest thing we can do is pray for and forgive those who hurt us and to let them off our hook.

WHAAAAAAAAAAAAAAAAAAAAAAT???!!!

Uncle Dug has to be kidding!! Forgive my bully?? Pray for him?? Let my hurts go?? That makes no sense at all! As far as I'm concerned, Mugersnot got everything he deserved. I told Uncle Dug that wasn't going to work for me.

Praying is something I'm not sure really works. I'm not interested in hearing anything about praying for my enemy or going down on my knees. The only thing I want to know is what the ancient dude did to bust his bullies with that incredible secret. Uncle Dug said he understood my feelings and that forgiving is not always easy, but the Heavenly King gives us grace to forgive those who hurt us and to pray for good things to happen to them. I'm going to have to think about that.

At BT time, Uncle Dug reminded George and me how vicious and determined Nehemiah's bullies were in trying to stop the rebuilding of the wall and gates. I thought of Mugersnot, who would like nothing more than to stop me from finishing my science project.

119

Uncle Dug said the Israelites were getting discouraged. The taunting and teasing from their bullies were wearing them down, so they started complaining to each other, saying they would never complete the wall. Uncle Dug told George and me that this happened because the Israelites had taken their eyes off the Heavenly King and what He could do to help. They gave in to their fears and started singing a gripe and grumble song:

"Rubble rubble everywhere,
Double **trouble,** wear and tear,
Grumble **mumble,** me oh my,
we'll never build this wall up high!"

With the Israelites singing the blues, the bullies took advantage and pressed harder with more snickering, and they cooked up an evil plan to wipe them out, telling them, "You Israelites will be swooped down on and taken out, and the work will be stopped."

But Nehemiah sent some loyal Israelites close to where the bullies lived. One day, one of the Israelites overheard the bullies' plan to swoop in from every direction to attack and destroy them. After hearing the evil plot, Nehemiah placed armed guards behind the lowest parts of the wall and stationed some Israelites to stand guard in their family groups with swords, spears, and bows. Then Nehemiah called a meeting with the nobles and the rest of the Israelites and encouraged them not to be afraid of the enemy. He told them, "Remember the Heavenly King is with you; fight for your families and your homes!"

120

George said he would feel really bad if bullies were tearing into him all the time. Uncle Dug told us Nehemiah didn't allow the words of his enemies to stick in his mind and heart to discourage him. He had been given an important job by the Heavenly King and he was confident that he would be given the strength and wisdom to finish that job. He would not let mean words have power to hurt him and stop the work on the wall and gates.

I thought of Mugersnot and how many times I let his cruel words hurt me. I suppose I could try and do what Nehemiah did and have confidence in the Heavenly King, but I don't know if I'm ready for that. Mean words have discouraged me even though I know they're not always true.

Uncle Dug said mean words can be used like a weapon but we don't have to believe or fear them. Instead, we can always know we are loved and valuable in the eyes of the Heavenly King, who cares and watches over us. That's the truth that really counts.

What Uncle Dug told me next was frustrating and radical. The truth bomb was dropped again! He said that no matter how bad Mugersnot treats me, I should forgive him and always treat him with kindness, truth, and respect! "Hurt people hurt people," Uncle Dug said. Maybe Mugersnot's words are coming from his own pain. Uncle Dug went on to say how showing kindness is one of the most powerful weapons to use against our enemies. "Pray for them and be kind to them, and they'll have a hard time staying your enemy."

WHAAAAAAAAAAAAAAAAAAAAAAT???!!!

I asked Uncle Dug if Nehemiah did that to his bullies. He said, "Yes, he did. Nehemiah didn't plot revenge, he challenged his enemies with the truth. Holding to the truth is kind and good and ends up helping everyone."

Mugersnot deserves payback. So far I've lived by the rule "Don't get mad; get even," and I've had such a good time humiliating him in Mr. Bullard's class. Uncle Dug is going too far. He's saying to give your bully what they don't deserve by giving them grace, kindness, truth, and respect. George thought Uncle Dug's idea was great. That's easy for him to say because he doesn't have Mugersnot in his life.

I need to do some **real** thinking about what I am being **asked** to do.

George asked what Nehemiah was going to do next. Uncle Dug said the Israelites kept on rebuilding the wall but they kept their guard up. Half of them stood firm in their armor, holding their spears, shields, and bows. The other half worked to finish the wall, but even they had swords strapped to their waists or held weapons in their empty hands while they worked. Nehemiah kept a trumpeter with him at all times to sound the alarm if the enemy appeared. If the Israelites heard the trumpet, they were to drop their tools, run to the sound of the blast, and be courageous, knowing the Heavenly King would fight for them.

Uncle Dug told George and me that Nehemiah and the Israelites worked from sunrise to sunset and posted guards to watch through the night. They knew the bullies would seize any chance to come against them. Nehemiah also asked everyone living outside the city to sleep inside the walls of Jerusalem at night. He needed their help protecting the workers. While the building was going on, the Israelites were so dedicated they not only had their weapons with them every moment, but they also didn't take time to bathe or change their clothes.

• • • • • • • • • • •

George said he thought the Israelites would have smelled terrible, like a garbage can full of rotting bananas. I didn't agree. I told him they would have stunk as bad as Mugersnot's stinky armpits. George said,

"No! They would have smelled as bad as dead grasshoppers."

I insisted that the Israelites would have stunk as bad as Mugersnot's sticker-peeling breath. That's when Uncle Dug interrupted and said with a smile, "The Israelites smelled as bad as this!" He waved his pillow over his backside, and a powerful stench made George and me almost pass out. All of us couldn't stop laughing and we had to open the window just so we could get to sleep.

Gone Fishin'

I lost my journal this morning. I looked everywhere. I was so bummed and couldn't focus on much else. I sent a prayer up to the Heavenly King about getting it back. Then, after dinner, Buckles jumped up on my bed carrying my journal in his slobbery mouth. He dropped it on top of my covers. It had a ton of dirt all over it. Buckles must have buried it somewhere in the yard, like one of his bones. I wiped it off and except for a few teeth marks and saliva stains, it still looked pretty good. From now on...

...I'll hide it in my **dresser** drawer or in my backpack where **Buckles** won't be able to get it.

I was thinking yesterday that if Buckles hadn't brought it back, it's likely it would have turned into an ancient manuscript. Maybe somebody in a few thousand years would find my doodles and writing interesting and my journal would end up in the British Museum.

Uncle Dug promised to take George and me fishing. He's leaving for Israel on Tuesday, so this is our last weekend with him. It's a good thing Mom slept late. She's not selling her potholders at the farmer's market this morning because she ran out and needs to crochet more. George and I usually help her by setting up her table. I taped a sign on the refrigerator so Mom would know where we were. It said, Gone Fishin'.

Uncle Dug, George, and I headed out, and, of course, Buckles came along too. We didn't get any action on our lines for a long time. When we were feeling really frustrated, Uncle Dug told us that we had to have faith like Nehemiah. The next thing we knew, George and I were catching the biggest fish of our lives. I snagged a brook trout that measured twenty-six inches and George caught a bluegill and that dude measured thirteen and a half inches.

Both George and I were thrilled. I told Uncle Dug we were lucky to catch fish that big. He said our big catch was not because of luck, but was an answer to his prayer.

We took our catch, put them on ice, and moved to the other side of the lake to get a change of scenery. We found a large, flat rock that overlooked the lake. We dropped our fishing lines and waited for a couple of big yanks. It didn't happen. I told Uncle Dug I had faith and it still didn't happen. But what seemed almost better than reeling in another big one was that I felt okay with what I had already caught.

The sights around us were pretty amazing. Lots of green pine trees, yellow wildflowers, and sparkling blue water, and a deer or two scampered through the grass. After a while, George asked Uncle Dug if he would finish telling us the story of Nehemiah.

Uncle Dug told us that discouragement for the Israelites didn't just come from the tricky trio. The Israelites themselves began to complain that they were having to work on the wall instead of working in their own fields and vineyards. Families were going hungry and had to sell their property to survive. Some of them even sold their kids into slavery! Many of these poor Israelites had to borrow money from their rich relatives, nobles, and officials. To make it all worse, they were charged extra fees to borrow that money.

George asked, "Why were they charged extra feet?" "It's 'fees,' not 'feet!'" I told him. Uncle Dug said, "The Israelites were forced to pay extra fees just to get the money they needed to feed their families." George said that wasn't fair and I agreed. I couldn't believe how greedy some of the rich Israelites were in Nehemiah's day.

I asked Uncle Dug what was done to help the poor Israelites. He told me that since Nehemiah was the governor of Judah, he called a meeting with the nobles and officials. He told them they were very wrong to charge extra and that he had never charged his fellow Israelites fees if they needed to borrow money. Nehemiah also reminded them that he didn't take a governor's salary and...

...he fed **150** officials at his **table** every day, including visitors from other lands.

Nehemiah demanded that charging extra fees to fellow Israelites be stopped immediately and that all the excess money charged so far be returned to the poor borrowers. The rich Israelites said they would do it. Nehemiah got tough and made them swear to it. George interrupted, asking, "Oh, does that mean it was like a pinky promise and cross my heart?" Uncle Dug said, "No, they had to really keep their word or there would be some serious consequences." Uncle Dug patted George on the head. Maybe he knew that George didn't really keep his pinky promises.

Uncle Dug said that when Nehemiah cracked down on the greedy rich, the people didn't have to worry about their fields or their families anymore.

This **freed** them up to continue working on the **wall** and **gates** of the city.

I was glad Nehemiah stood up for the poor Israelites. It made me think about what happened last year to our family. I overheard Mom talking on the phone to a relative who had more money than he could spend. Mom was sick and missed several days of work. She asked him whether he would help us out with our rent for just a month. We got the money, but we were charged extra and Mom wasn't happy about that. She scrambles working a couple of jobs to make ends meet, and it's not fair that she has to pay extra just to borrow one month's rent. The poor Israelites in Nehemiah's day must have really felt like Mom did. I wondered why Mom didn't ask Uncle Dug. He would have helped her out for free. I guess he was probably out of the country.

When it was all over, Mom decided to start selling her potholders at the farmer's market to earn extra money for emergency savings.

Uncle Dug said the sun was getting low, so we'd better be heading home and he would tell us the rest of Nehemiah's story before he left.

I picked up my two-foot **trout**, and it **crossed** my mind for a second...

...that maybe prayer really did have something to do with me snagging it.

Mom couldn't believe that George and I caught such huge fish. She and Aunt Gertie cooked them up after we cleaned them.

We had one of the best dinners we've had in a long time. Aunt Gertie put some kind of serious and tasty seasoning on our prized fish. She made sure every inch of it was covered by sticking the fish in a plastic bag with the seasoning and shaking it up. When she was done shaking it, Aunt Gertie put the fish in the oven and baked it. She called our dinner "Snag it, Shake it, Bake it." George thought that was funny so he started running around the table shaking his finger and saying over and over, "Snag it, shake it, bake it!"

By the time we all went to bed, we were too tired for any of Uncle Dug's BT time. At the last minute, George got a second wind and wanted to stay up and hear more about Nehemiah. That didn't happen because Mom came into my room and took George back to his hammock. I fell asleep thinking about how amazing it was that I caught the biggest fish of my life.

The Air Had Been Sucked Out of Me

I woke up smelling bacon this morning. Uncle Dug was in the kitchen making breakfast. After downing about a dozen pancakes soaked in blueberry syrup, I wanted to play some video games, but Uncle Dug said that I could go to church with him, Aunt Gertie, and George. I wasn't up for that so I went outside and shot a few hoops and then worked on my science project. I had a second breakfast after Mom woke up and gave her a few of Uncle Dug's awesome pancakes. I'm sure going to miss his cooking after he's gone.

Once everyone got home from church, Uncle Dug took a look at my progress on my science project and said it was coming along nicely. He thought my design for my Mars huts was pretty cool. Later on, George wanted to get some pizza, so Uncle Dug took us all out to get some. Afterwards we went to Doodle Dud's Creamery and I ate another huge banana split.

George had a junior-sized one and he still couldn't finish it.

At BT time tonight, George asked if the tricky trio was going to come up with a trick to throw Nehemiah off his groove. Uncle Dug told us that two of the trio, Sanballat and Geshem, wanted to meet with Nehemiah, but the truth was they wanted to hurt him. That didn't happen because the Heavenly King gave Nehemiah wisdom, and he saw through their tricky plans. The bullies lied to him four times to try to trap him. It didn't work. The fifth time, Sanballat and Geshem sent a letter to Nehemiah. It was full of lies. They said there were rumors that the only reason he was building the wall was to set himself up as the new king of Jerusalem. Then they asked Nehemiah if he would come over and talk with them about these rumors. They said he was in danger and if Nehemiah didn't go along with the meeting, his stubbornness would be reported to King Artie, who would be very angry and would make trouble for Nehemiah and the Israelites. But Nehemiah knew it was all a set-up to get him to stop work on the wall.

I thought of **Mugersnot** and how he would stoop to **lie** about me and be **tricky** too, if it meant he could win the **science fair** and take first place.

Nehemiah confronted Sanballat and Geshem and told them he knew there wasn't any truth in their letter and they were making the whole thing up. An Israelite who was a spy for the tricky trio even warned Nehemiah, "If you don't run and hide in the temple of the Heavenly King, you'll be killed." Nehemiah figured out quickly that it was a fake-out since this Israelite was being paid off by Sanballat and Tobiah!

131

The last thing the tricky trio tried to do to stop the work was to send a bunch of nasty letters Nehemiah's way to discourage and threaten him,....

...just like the **mean** notes that Mugersnot has been **spreading** around about me in Mr. Bullard's classroom.

Nehemiah just prayed again that the Heavenly King would make his hands strong to continue the work.

George said Nehemiah was no "fraidy cat." Nehemiah was not scared off by his bullies with their tricks and lies. He stood up to them by speaking truth with grace and doing what was right. Despite those bullies, Nehemiah and the families in Jerusalem, including the nobles and officials, worked hard together to accomplish a huge goal. On October 2, 445 BC, the wall and gates of Jerusalem were finished—only fifty-two days after the work was first begun.

Not a gap was left and the frames for all the gates were put in.

Uncle Dug said Nehemiah's bullies and the surrounding nations were frightened and humiliated by this accomplishment. They realized that the work had been done with the help of the Heavenly King, because it had been finished so fast.

I looked over at George. He was already asleep. I sat up straight in my bunk and asked Uncle Dug, "Wait, that's it? The end? What about the incredible secret? What about the Bully Buster?"

I had been **hoping** to hear something really **amazing** and way out of the **ordinary.**

I asked Uncle Dug again, "So what's the incredible secret?"

Uncle Dug said one word: "Prayer."

I was shocked and underwhelmed.

Then I remembered how Nehemiah prayed and how Uncle Dug also thought I should pray for Mugersnot to heal quickly.

I didn't **know** what to say. I was **confused.**

Uncle Dug reminded me that Nehemiah prayed before he asked King Artie to travel to Jerusalem. Because he prayed, the Heavenly King gave him favor with King Artie.

Nehemiah prayed for strength and wisdom to deal with his bullies. The Heavenly King gave Nehemiah the right words to use against the tricky trio and sent him people to warn him. The Heavenly King also used Nehemiah's prayer to send His special messengers to encourage him and the Israelites. When the wall workers got tired and Nehemiah prayed for strength, the Heavenly King answered and the wall was built and the gates set up in record time!

Uncle Dug saw *my* disappointment and told me to "cheer up," because I had no idea how powerful a weapon prayer is for the person who believes in the Heavenly King and talks to Him. Real prayer unleashes power, wisdom, and favor on the person praying and on the people and circumstances you're praying about. I wasn't sure how all that worked.

What Uncle Dug was telling me was hard to understand, let alone believe.

Then I asked him another question, not sure I wanted a second disappointing answer.

"So what about the Bully Buster? Who or what is he?"

That's when I was doubly blown away. Uncle Dug answered, "Andy, the Bully Buster is the one and only Heavenly King, the awesome Creator of everyone and everything. Nehemiah is a bully buster because he knows the Bully Buster. Through the power of the incredible secret we are able to connect with the Heavenly King. We also learn wisdom about bully busting by reading His words in the ancient book, the Bible."

After hearing what he said, I felt like the air had been sucked out of me.

It really wasn't the answer I was expecting.

How do prayer and the ancient book help me with Mugersnot? The truth is, I'm let down. I imagined the Bully Buster would be some fantastic superhero who would show up by *my* side and fight *my* battles with me. I looked over at George, who was still fast asleep. I don't think he heard a thing. Even if he had, he wouldn't have had a problem with it because whatever Uncle Dug says, George gobbles up, no questions asked.

Without saying anything else, Uncle Dug climbed the ladder to *my* bunk, scooped up George, and carried him to his hammock.

When he came back to *my* room, I pretended to be asleep.

134

Last Supper

Mugersnot shot a bunch of rubber bands at me today when Mr. Bullard wasn't looking. When he turned around, I got stern looks because he thought I was doing it. I wanted to blurt out, "It's Mugersnot!" But I didn't. I'm so over Mugersnot and his antics. He also shoved his crutch into the back of my chair. I almost shoved it back, but I didn't. My mind is still whirring over what Uncle Dug told me last night.

Tonight was the last supper with Uncle Dug, and the surprising thing is Aunt Polly came. She never likes going anywhere except to the cat shelter to volunteer. Uncle Dug's plane flies out early tomorrow morning.

Once George **realized** that Uncle Dug was really leaving, he **stuck** to him like glue, following him **everywhere**, even when he went outside to dump the trash.

George asked if he could give Uncle Dug his best grasshopper as a going-away gift. Uncle Dug didn't take him up on it but he did say it was a nice thought. I didn't think so.

After dinner, we went to the living room and Aunt Gertie served us apple pie, and it was amazing. She's a pretty good cook as long as she doesn't get distracted. It had a big scoop of vanilla ice cream on top. I wished Aunt Gertie had pulled this kind of pie off for Flynn when I was trying to convince him to make the bully-busting video.

135

When we were ready for bed, Uncle Dug told George and me the last of Nehemiah's story. We did the final BT time, and George promised, crossed his fingers, and said he didn't have any grasshoppers, so I let him join us.

Because I knew the incredible secret, and who the Bully Buster is, and George knew too (because I told him), I let Uncle Dug know that I wasn't interested in hearing more of Nehemiah's story.

But Uncle Dug wouldn't let me off the hook.

He started by saying that the word got out fast that Jerusalem was now the happening place. More and more exiles were returning to Jerusalem, almost fifty thousand. The broken wall and gates had been restored, but now the broken lives of the followers of the Heavenly King needed to be restored too. Uncle Dug told us that the Israelites did some serious owning up to their rebellious ways. Six days after the wall was finished, Nehemiah gathered all the people inside the wall to hear Ezra, the High Priest, read aloud from the wise rules of the Heavenly King. Ezra stood on a platform above the crowd and read from early morning until noon. Men, women, and children listened closely.

George said that no kid would ever listen to rules for that long. I thought so too.

The Israelites began to praise the Heavenly King, the great and awesome Creator. They lifted their hands, bowed down, and worshiped with their faces to the ground. Then the other teachers helped Ezra by clearly explaining the meaning of the wise rules to the Israelites.

Uncle Dug told George and me that when the Israelites heard the Heavenly King's rules, they were super sad over how many of them they had broken. They hadn't cared for others like they should have; they had forgotten about the poor, and they had made up other gods. They couldn't stop weeping and howling. George interrupted Uncle Dug, saying how bad he would have felt if he were one of those Israelites who disappointed and hurt the Heavenly King. Then George told me that he was sorry that he had lied to me so many times about not having grasshoppers at bedtime when he really did. I told him that I was glad he was sorry and in the future he better prove his "I'm sorry" by not doing it again. George gave me a hug. I hugged him back. I don't remember the last time...

...we gave each other a real **bro hug** instead of doing it just because Mom **told** us to.

Uncle Dug went on and said how Nehemiah told the Israelites they shouldn't be full of tears anymore because the day was special and they should be celebrating all the good things the Heavenly King had given them. He also reminded the Israelites that the joy of the Heavenly King was their strength.

Then Uncle Dug turned on the light, reached into his backpack, and brought out wrapped sweet cakes and cookies from Israel. He told us he had been waiting to give these to us and the time had arrived. George jumped off my bunk and eagerly took the sweets from Uncle Dug. Then he remembered to toss a few up to me. Uncle Dug laughed and said that George had the spirit of joy and celebration that the Israelites had. They knew the Heavenly King had shown His love and kindness by restoring them to their promised land, rebuilding their temple—their place of worship—and finally sending Nehemiah to rebuild Jerusalem's crumbled wall and burned gates. Now that they heard the words of the Heavenly King and understood how far they had fallen, they had a new determination to follow His wise rules.

I asked Uncle Dug if Nehemiah and the Israelites threw a celebration party once the wall was finished. They did, and it lasted a week. Then the Israelites appreciated their true Heavenly King even more. They praised Him for how good, merciful, just, powerful, wise, and strong He is. Then Uncle Dug read Nehemiah's "hip-hip-hooray" words from the Bible. It was about the Heavenly King and His awesomeness. I tried to remember them. They went something like this:

Your name, Heavenly King, is the best name ever. You alone are fantastic and have made the heavens and every star, the Earth and everything on it (even Buckles). You also made the seas and all the fish and weird creatures. Somehow, by your power, You keep them all going.

Now I get it! It's the Heavenly King who made the stars and the universe.

So, He's the "Someone" I've wondered about on my amazing stargazing adventures with Buckles.

Uncle Dug closed the ancient book. The story of Nehemiah was over. That ancient dude got me thinking deeper for sure, and I think he got George thinking deeper too, because this time, George kept his promise. After he left my room, I carefully checked my pillow and under the sheets. There wasn't one beady-eyed grasshopper staring back at me!

He's Gone

He's gone. After school today, George and I got to drop Uncle Dug off at the airport. Believe it or not, we both got in the old T with Aunt Gertie again. She didn't roll through a stop sign, hit a parked car, or run into a fire hydrant. Her driving lessons have helped.

When **Uncle Dug** got out of the car to give George and me our **final** hug,

I couldn't believe that I teared up. Uncle Dug slipped a small wrapped package into my backpack and told me to check it out later. It's a good thing George didn't see him do it, because he would have wanted one too. Uncle Dug told George and me he'll be back next summer to take us to the Badlands of South Dakota on a dinosaur dig. I can't wait! George said, "I'm already packed!"

140

Mugersnot was still limping around in a leg cast and crutches today. After passing him in the hallway, he glared at me and said, "Have a nice trip," and stuck out his crutch to trip me.

But I was quick and jumped over it.

I thought about how Nehemiah didn't let his bullies get to him. I decided to just let it go and move on fast. I knew it was the right move to make.

I still don't have a clue what Mugersnot is doing for his science project or what was in the big box he was carrying when he fell on the stairs. I guess I'll know soon enough if it has something to do with the science fair. I can't believe it's only three days away.

Everyone Was Buzzing

Mugersnot started in with his BEEP-BEEP-BEEPing when he saw me in the hallway this morning, but I wasn't bugged by it this time. I smiled at him and went on to Mr. Bullard's class. Everyone was buzzing about the science fair and how it was only a couple of days away. I felt good about my project and I only had to print out my geodesic domes, connecting tubes, and the bricks for my wall on the 3D printer. Then I'll be ready for my presentation to the judges. Mr. Bullard told me I could come in after school tomorrow to use the printer. He wouldn't be there, but his assistant would. On my way out of the classroom, Mugersnot stopped me and asked if I was ready for the judging. I told him I would be as soon as my domes, tubes, and bricks were printed.

He gave me a **strange** smile.

I called Flynn when I got home from school and told him about my run-in with Mugersnot. He said to be careful around him and to try and stay focused so that I would finish strong with my project. I asked Flynn if he could come over so we could talk about what I was doing with my Mars colony. He came over and we snacked on Cheezebitzies while I told him all about it. He liked what I had done and cautioned me to hurry up and get my 3D printing done. I thought of Nehemiah's enemies doing everything they could do to stop his mission to rebuild Jerusalem's wall and repair the gates.

I'm nervous about Mugersnot trying to sabotage my project.

Tonight I **lay down** on my bunk and **stared** up at the popcorn ceiling.

I closed my eyes and had an honest talk with the Bully Buster. I guess you could say I wielded the incredible secret: I prayed. When I was almost finished, I heard a quiet voice say, "Be chill, I got your back." I wasn't sure what that was all about so I opened my eyes and looked around. That's when I saw my backpack lying on my bed with a small package peeking out from it. It was Uncle Dug's gift! I hurriedly unwrapped it and found the ancient book, a pocket-sized Bible just like his! I opened it and saw his handwriting on the inside cover.

To ANDY, this is the Best Book I CAN GIVE YOU. the SWORD of TRUTH Be Sure To Read it To YouR BRoTHER GEORGE. Love, UNCLE DUG

P.S. Fight your **bullies** by walking in the power of the incredible secret because the Bully Buster is **always** with you. He's got your back. Don't forget **Nehemiah 8:10.** I have it bookmarked for you."

I went to the verse and read, "The joy of the Lord is your strength!"

Refill Pellet Container

When I went to print out my domes, tubes, and bricks on the 3D printer, an error message came up: REFILL PELLET CONTAINER. I went to the cabinet where Mr. Bullard stores the plastic pellets, ...

...but it was **empty** except for some **magnets** and a small pocketknife.

Mr. Bullard's assistant and I also checked the cupboards and drawers in the classroom. No pellets were found. I called Mr. Bullard. He was surprised that the pellets were missing because there were six bags yesterday. I told him the cabinet had nothing in it except for a few magnets and a pocket knife. He wondered about the knife and asked me to leave it in his desk. When I went back to get it, I saw the initials TM etched on its handle. Tommy Mugersnot. One of my worst nightmares had come true.

It looked like **Mugersnot** had **sabotaged** my project, and my heart **dropped** to my feet.

Then it dropped below the floor after I called Mr. Bullard back and asked him about getting more pellets. He said that he orders them online and it would take about a week for them to arrive. Judging begins tomorrow, which means my Mars project is doomed! I wanted to throw a dozen eggs at Mugersnot's house.

I left the classroom, and on my way out, I noticed a note lying on top of my desk. ...

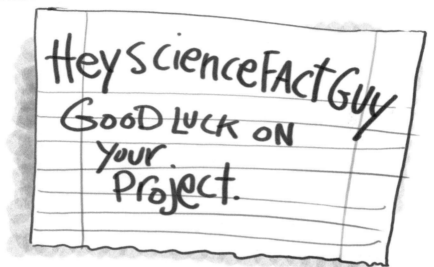

Hey ScienceFactGuy
Good luck on your Project.

I crumpled the note, shoved it in my pocket, and left. Mugersnot had gone to a new level. I didn't know what I was going to do.

My enemy had triumphed. I wanted to give up. But then I thought about something Uncle Dug told me during our BT time. Nehemiah, the ancient dude, crashed through quitting points with the power of the incredible secret. Didn't I talk to the Bully Buster last night? I could do it again, right at this moment. I didn't have a lot of words to say except "HELP!"

When I got to my house, I knew I needed to call Flynn. He answered right away and he wasn't surprised when I told him what Mugersnot had done. Flynn said he would come right over and help me figure out a way to save my project.

145

Flynn lived out the meaning of best friend. He worked with me for hours, putting together my domes and bricks. They may not be perfect or close to what I planned, but they will do the job. We made the domes from foil cupcake holders, which was easy because we just turned them upside down, and we made the bricks for the wall around the colony from sugar cubes covered with aluminum foil. We used empty paper towel holders for the connecting tubes. All this took a lot of time. We wrapped almost a hundred cubes with foil. I stumbled on the idea while hunting for a snack for Flynn and me. Mom had put the cupcake holders next to the box of Cheezebitzies. While Flynn and I munched away on our favorite snack, we glued both the cupcake holders and foil bricks onto my presentation board.

After it was done, Flynn and I thought our work was pretty good, even though the 3D-printed geodesic domes and bricks would have been a lot better. But at this point, I'm okay with what I have and...

...I'm as prepared as I can be.

After Flynn left, Buckles came into my room, and I took that to mean that he wanted to do a little amazing gazing. As tired as I was, I grabbed a blanket to sit on and went out with him to the backyard. I didn't bring my telescope. I wanted to look at the stars straight up. There's something about doing that which feels kind of special, and I wasn't disappointed. The twinkling night-lights were super brilliant tonight. I couldn't get enough of their wonder, even though I was struggling to keep Mugersnot and what he'd done out of my head. I took another long look at the stars. They now seem way cooler because I know the Bully Buster created them. From now on, I'm going to ask for wisdom, just like Nehemiah did, to handle my bullies. I'm pretty sure my 'Help' prayer was heard this afternoon and my prayer from last night too, because I'm feeling chill about my problems with Mugersnot.

Buckles and I continued staring up for a long while until my neck started hurting. Then we both lay down on the blanket and fell asleep. I woke up when I heard Mom calling my name.

"Andy, where are you? Are you okay?"

I yelled back and told her I was fine. I really am.

Science Fair

The judging is over, and I didn't come in first. I came in third. But I did the best I could. Even if I'd had my 3D geodesic domes and bricks for my wall printed out perfectly, it wouldn't have made that much of a difference. It's kind of weird, but winning the science fair isn't as important to me anymore. But donuts still are, and I'm bummed that Miss Diddle forgot to bring them this year for the kids who turned in their projects.

A new kid took first. He had an interesting project about making small robots using the head of a toothbrush, a battery, and a small motor. He used a straight-bristle head and a slanted one and raced them against each other to see which one went fastest.

He called them
T-Brush Racers.

The surprising thing was Mugersnot didn't show up with his project. I found out that when he fell with his box down the stairs, small bottles of chemicals packed in it had shattered and destroyed everything inside. Some kids said Mugersnot was super ticked because he didn't have a chance to recover his project in time for judging. Even if he had gotten more chemicals, they needed several days to react. Since he couldn't enter the science fair, he wanted to make sure I couldn't either. He chose his usual, bullying way, got mad, and stole the pellets.

The same kids told me that Mugersnot was furious when he learned that I had come up with another idea for making the domes, bricks, and connecting tubes so I could still present to the judges. The kids warned me that nothing was going to stop Mugersnot from making trouble for me. They were right. When the judging was over and I was getting ready to leave, I heard,

"BEEP-BEEP-BEEP-GEEEEEEK!"

I turned around and saw Mugersnot hobbling on his crutches, making his way towards my project. He was struggling hard to carry a large plastic jug of milk in one of his hands.

I didn't have to be a **nuclear** physicist to know what his **nasty** plan was.

I got super mad and, without thinking, I charged at Mugersnot. He flinched and lost his grip on the milk jug. It fell to the floor with a thud and popped the jug's cap off, sending a gush of milk all over his face and clothes. As the jug began to empty on the floor, he reached down to pick it up but his crutch slipped and he fell down splat in the middle of the milk puddle. I stopped right before I got to him. The worst bully in the universe was lying on the ground at my feet, stunned, with small droplets of milk dripping from his chin.

A crowd of kids quickly gathered at the scene. One of them picked up the jug with the leftover milk, handed it to me and said, "Finish him off, Andy!" I looked down at Mugersnot. This was the moment I had been waiting for. Sweet revenge. He glared hard at me and I glared back harder. I had had enough of his taunts, torments, and terribleness! I started to tilt the jug, then froze. I remembered something Uncle Dug told me: "Sometimes, the bravest thing we can do is forgive."

I suddenly realized, if I took my revenge and got even, I was no better than Mugersnot, just one bully against another. Pouring the milk on him would make me a hero to the kids around but I would know in my heart that my anger and revenge were just me being scared. But I didn't have to be scared. I had the Bully Buster on my side, which meant I could forgive my enemy.

I handed the jug to one of the kids and reached my hand out to Mugersnot. He pushed it away and snapped, "I don't need your help!" I picked up his crutches and let him know I was sorry for charging and startling him. I offered my hand again. He grabbed it and then took his crutches from me. He steadied himself and hobbled away grunting, ...

"You're nothing but a wimp, Jones!"

Flynn dropped me off at my house. While we were in his car, he told me how bummed he was that he couldn't have been at the science fair to see the whole messy scene. Flynn thought I should have poured the last of the milk over Mugersnot. I told him that forgiveness and not playing the "get-even" game is the better way. He wasn't sure about that. I told him that even though it seems crazy, I'm becoming more convinced that it's true. I also let Flynn know that I felt bad for Mugersnot and what happened to his project. Flynn said I was "nuts" to feel that way. But if I'm nuts, Uncle Dug is too, and I don't think that's the case.

Once I got home, George met me at the door and held out his hand full of grasshoppers. He must have felt my disappointment about Mugersnot's sabotage and coming in third place. I guess he was trying to make me feel better. Aunt Gertie was in the kitchen and asked me how the judging went. I said, "It was fair and I did my best." Then she hugged me and said she had

150

just finished baking my favorite apple pie and we could eat it now instead of after dinner. She told me she was sorry that there wouldn't be any ice cream because George got to it first and finished it off. I looked over at George. He gave me a sly smile. "That's okay," I said. "There's a lot more to life than getting all the ice cream you want."

He **didn't** get it because he said, "You mean there's **more** ice cream?"

Saturday
may 20
Thinking a
Whole Lot Deeper

I woke up this morning feeling like everything is going to be okay. I'm really thinking a whole lot deeper about a whole lot of things and because of that, I've got some "takeaways" or "lessons learned," as Aunt Gertie says.

My first takeaway is that even if history feels ancient and not important, the lessons from a long time ago can teach you about life and what's really right. You gotta dig a little deeper to find the truth. Once you get it, it shouldn't just stay glued in your head, but you should live it out. Now that I'm reading the ancient book, it's beginning to make sense in ways I never thought it would.

That's probably because my attitude about it changed. What I learned from Uncle Dug about archaeology has made...

...the ancient book seem more believable and helped build my trust in it.

My second takeaway is that giving grace and being kind is way better than getting even with someone who hurts or disappoints you. Showing kindness to the nastiest person around you isn't easy. It only gets a little easier if you understand that everyone, even the worst ones, are fighting some kind of battle—that's what Uncle Dug says.

My final takeaway is that prayer matters and it really works. It is the incredible secret because you're talking to the One and Only Heavenly King, who knows how things should be. He is the Creator of everyone and everything. Since He made all of it, He knows best how to bust a bully and that's why He's the Bully Buster.

As far as Mugersnot goes, I don't think he'll be changing very much any time soon. He'll probably still pass nasty notes about me, breathe down my neck in class, kick my chair, throw milk and Twinkie bombs my way, trip me in the hall, and do other bully stuff. I'm pretty sure when Flynn and the kids at school see me ignore Mugersnot, they'll be shocked because they'll expect me to feed the "get-even wolf." But I'm not going to. As tough as it might be, I'll put my feet where my mouth is and do good to Mugersnot, because the Heavenly King cares about his problems just as much as he cares about mine.

After school yesterday, Mr. Bullard asked me to meet with him and Mugersnot in the principal's office. The rumor was that Mugersnot was facing a suspension for stealing the pellets and bringing a knife to school.

When I got there, Mugersnot was in the room, and so was Principal Carter. Mugersnot looked pretty roughed up. Mr. Bullard told him he needed to follow through on what they talked about. Mugersnot stared at the floor and said, "Sorry for sabotaging your project, Jones." I told him I forgave him and I wasn't going to hold it against him. Principal Carter turned to talk quietly with Mr. Bullard. That's when Mugersnot glared at me and mouthed the words, "You rat!" I didn't say anything. Mr. Bullard turned back and told Mugersnot, "You should be happy. We've decided not to suspend you this time, Tommy. But if you do something like this again, you're out of Woodside." Mugersnot didn't look relieved about getting off. He only muttered, "Sure, thanks."

When Mugersnot and I left the office, I asked him if he had returned the pellets. He said they were trashed, but his dad would pay for them because his family wasn't poor like mine. Right away, I clenched my fist and almost slugged him. But I didn't. Instead, what came out of my mouth surprised me.

I told Mugersnot how I was sorry to hear about the bottles in his box being shattered and how disappointed he must have been. Mugersnot opened his eyes wide like he couldn't believe what I'd said. He opened them wider when I reached into my backpack and held out a new journal. I told him how writing in it every day had helped me figure some things out and I hoped it could help him too. This journal was for him.

I'm seriously thinking about starting an after-school club. I'll call it "Bully

He paused for a few seconds, then snatched it and took off.

Busters." I want to learn more about the Bully Buster, the ancient book, and the incredible secret, and I want other kids to be able to learn more too. If everyone pulls on the same side of the rope, maybe we can make a difference for kids who are facing their own bullies. After all, life should be about caring for others, even the creepy crawlers who get under your skin. But those types won't be bugging me as much anymore, thanks to the power of the incredible secret and to...

...the most AWESOME
BULLY BUSTER!

The End!

MEET THE AUTHOR

Annie Winston, a former Doublemint Gum twin, loves writing fun stories for kids. She's not only a winning author but an inspiring speaker. Annie has spoken to thousands of elementary students with heartfelt messages of dreaming big, never giving up, and character counts. She also stresses to students the importance of working hard to develop their unique gifts and talents so they might become the best version of themselves.

anniewinston.com

MEET THE ILLUSTRATOR

Gary Locke has never lost a foot race to Brad Pitt. (True Story!) When he's not chasing his gorgeous wife around, he's running races, drawing pictures, raising kids, enjoying his grandkids, and playing disc golf. He is married to the Homecoming Queen. He saw her FIRST! BACK OFF! Get your OWN!!! She is his. END OF STORY!

Garyartgood.com

Here are
some pages
you can
journal on!

Day 1 _____

_____

_____

_____

_____

_____

_____

_____

_____

_____

Day 2 _____

_____

_____

_____

_____

_____

_____

_____

_____

_____

_____

_____

_____

_____

Day 3 _____

_____

_____

_____

_____

_____

_____

_____

_____

_____

_____

_____

_____

_____

Day 4 _____

_____
_____
_____
_____
_____
_____
_____
_____
_____
_____
_____
_____
_____

Day 5 _____

_____
_____
_____
_____
_____
_____
_____
_____
_____
_____
_____
_____

Day 6 _____

_____
_____
_____
_____
_____
_____
_____
_____
_____
_____
_____
_____
_____
_____

Day 7 _____

_____
_____
_____
_____
_____
_____
_____
_____
_____
_____
_____
_____
_____
_____

Day 8 _____

_____

_____

_____

_____

_____

_____

_____

_____

_____

_____

_____

_____

_____

Day 9 _____

_____
_____
_____
_____
_____
_____
_____
_____
_____
_____
_____
_____
_____

Day 10 _____

_____

_____

_____

_____

_____

_____

_____

_____

_____

_____

_____

_____

Day 11 _____

_____

_____

_____

_____

_____

_____

_____

_____

_____

_____

_____

_____

_____

Day 12 _____

_____

_____

_____

_____

_____

_____

_____

_____

_____

_____

_____

_____

_____